Uncle Wiggily in Wonderland

Howard Roger Garis

Uncle Wiggily In Wonderland

CHAPTER I

UNCLE WIGGILY AND WONDERLAND ALICE

Once upon a time, after Uncle Wiggily Longears, the nice bunny rabbit gentleman, had some funny adventures with Baby Bunty, and when he found that his rheumatism did not hurt him so much as he hopped on his red, white and blue striped barber pole crutch, the bunny uncle wished he might have some strange and wonderful adventures.

"I think I'll just hop along and look for a few," said Uncle Wiggily to himself one morning. He twinkled his pink nose, and then he was all ready to start.

"Good-bye, Nurse Jane! Good-bye!" he called to his muskrat lady housekeeper, with whom he lived in a hollow stump bungalow. "I'm going to look for some wonderful adventures!" He hopped down the front steps, with his red, white and blue striped crutch under one paw, and his tall, silk hat on his head. "Good-bye, Miss Fuzzy Wuzzy!"

"Good-bye!" answered Nurse Jane. "I hope you have some nice adventures!"

"Thanks, I wish you the same," answered Uncle Wiggily, and away he went over the fields and through the woods. He had not hopped very far, looking this way and that, before, all of a sudden, he came to a queer little place, near an old rail fence. Down in one corner was a hole, partly underground.

"Ha! That's queer," said Uncle Wiggily to himself. "That looks just like the kind of an underground house, or burrow, where I used to live. I wonder if this can be where I made my home before I moved to the hollow stump bungalow? I must take a look. Nurse Jane would like to hear all about it."

So Uncle Wiggily, folding back his ears in order that they would not get bent over and broken, began crawling down the rabbit hole, for that is what it really was.

It was dark inside, but the bunny uncle did not mind that, being able to see in the dark. Besides, he could make his pink nose twinkle when he wanted to, and this gave almost as much light as a firefly.

"No, this isn't the burrow where I used to live," said Uncle Wiggily to himself, when he had hopped quite a distance into the hole. "But it's very nice. Perhaps I may have an adventure here. Who knows?"

And just as he said that to himself, Uncle Wiggily saw, lying under a little table, in what seemed to be a room of the underground house, a small glass box.

"Ha! My adventure begins!" cried Uncle Wiggily. "I'll open that glass box and see what is in it."

So the bunny uncle raised the cover, and in the glass box was a little cake, made of carrots and cabbage, and on top, spelled out in pink raisins, were the words:

"EAT ME!"

"Ha! That's just what I'll do!" cried jolly Uncle Wiggily, and, never stopping to think anything might be wrong, the bunny gentleman ate the cake. And then, all of a sudden, he began to feel very funny.

"Oh, my!" exclaimed Uncle Wiggily. "I hope that cake didn't belong to my nephew, Sammie Littletail, or Johnnie or Billie Bushytail, the squirrel brothers. One of them may have lost it out of his lunch basket on his way to school. I hope it wasn't any of their cake. But there is surely something funny about it, for I feel so very queer!"

And no wonder! For Uncle Wiggily had suddenly begun to grow very large. His ears grew taller, so that they lifted his tall silk hat right off his head. His legs seemed as long as bean poles, and as for his whiskers and pink, twinkling nose, they seemed so far away from his eyes that he wondered if he would ever get them near enough to see to comb the one, or scratch the other when it felt ticklish.

"This is certainly remarkable!" cried Uncle Wiggily. "I wonder what made me grow so large all of a sudden? Could it have been the cake which gave me the indyspepsia?"

"It was the cake!" cried a sudden and buzzing voice, and, looking around the hole Uncle Wiggily saw a big mosquito. "It was the cake that made you grow big," went on the bad biting bug, "and I put it here for you to eat."

"What for?" asked the bunny uncle, puzzled like.

"So you would grow so big that you couldn't get out of this hole," was the answer. "And now you can't! This is how I have caught you! Ha! Ha!" and the mosquito buzzed a most unpleasant laugh.

"Oh, dear!" thought Uncle Wiggily. "I wonder if I am caught? Can't I get out as I got in?"

Quickly he hopped to the front of the hole. But alas! Likewise sorrowfulness! He had grown so big from eating the magical cake that he could not possibly squeeze out of the hole through which he had crawled into the underground burrow.

"Now I have caught you!" cried the mosquito. "Since we could not catch you at your soldier tent or in the trenches near your hollow stump bungalow, I thought of this way. Now we have you and we'll bite you!" and the big mosquito, who with his bad friends had dug the hole on purpose to get Uncle Wiggily in a trap, began to play a bugle tune on his wings to call the other biting bugs.

"Oh, dear!" thought Uncle Wiggily. "I guess I am caught! And I haven't my talcum powder pop gun that shoots bean-bag bullets! Oh, if I could only get out of here!"

"You can get out, Uncle Wiggily," said a soft little voice down toward the end of his pink, twinkling nose. "You can get out!"

"Oh, no, I can't!" the bunny said. "I am much too large to squeeze out of the hole by which I came in here. Much too large. Oh, dear!"

"Here, drink some of this and you'll grow small just as I did when I drank from it before I fell into the pool of tears," the soft and gentle voice went on, and to Uncle Wiggily's surprise, there stood a nice little girl with long, flaxen hair. She was holding out to him a bottle with a tag that read:

"DRINK ME."

"Am I really to drink this?" asked the bunny.

"You are," said the little girl.

Uncle Wiggily took a long drink from the bottle. It tasted like lollypop ice cream soda, and no sooner had he taken a good sip than all of a sudden he found himself shutting up small, like a telescope. Smaller and smaller he shrank, until he was his own regular size, and then the little girl took him by the paw and cried:

"Come on! Now you can get out!"

And, surely enough, Uncle Wiggily could.

"But who are you?" he asked the little girl.

"Oh! I'm Alice from Wonderland," she said, "and I know you very well, though you never met me before. I'm in a book, but this is my holiday, so I came out. Come on, now, before the mosquitoes catch us! We'll have a lot of funny adventures with some friends of mine. Come on!" And away ran Uncle Wiggily with Wonderland Alice, who had saved him from being bitten. So everything came out all right, you see.

And if the teacup doesn't lose its handle and try to do a foxtrot waltz with the soup tureen, I'll tell you next about Uncle Wiggily and the March Hare.

CHAPTER II

UNCLE WIGGILY AND THE MARCH HARE

"Well, Uncle Wiggily, you certainly did have quite a time, didn't you," said Nurse Jane Fuzzy Wuzzy, the muskrat lady housekeeper for the rabbit gentleman as they both sat on the porch of the hollow stump bungalow one morning. It was the day after the bunny rabbit had been caught in the mosquito hole, where he swelled up too big to get out, after eating cake from the glass box, as I told you in the first story.

Then Alice from Wonderland happened along and gave Uncle Wiggily a drink from a magical little bottle so that he grew small enough to crawl out of the hole again.

"Yes, I had a wonderful time with Alice," said the rabbit gentleman. "It was quite an adventure."

"What do you s'pose was in the cake to make you swell up so large?" asked Nurse Jane.

"Cream puffs," answered Uncle Wiggily. "They're very swell-like, you know."

"Of course," agreed Nurse Jane. "And what was in the bottle to make you grow smaller?"

"Alum water," Uncle Wiggily made reply. "That's very shrinking, you know, and puckery."

"Of course," spoke Nurse Jane again, "I might have guessed it. Now I suppose you're off again?"

"Off to have another adventure," went on Uncle Wiggily, with a jolly laugh. "I hope I meet Alice again. I wonder where she lives?"

"Why, she's out of a book," said Nurse Jane. "I used to read about her to Sammie Littletail, when he was quite a little rabbit chap."

"Oh, yes, to be sure," said Uncle Wiggily. "Alice from Wonderland is like Mother Goose, Sinbad the Sailor and my other Arabian Night friends. Well, I hope I meet some of them and have another adventure now," and away he hopped down the front steps of his bungalow as spry as though he never had had the rheumatism.

The bad mosquitoes that used to live over in the swamp had gone away on their summer vacation, and so they did not bother the bunny rabbit just at present. He no longer had to practice being a soldier and stand on guard against them.

Pretty soon, as Uncle Wiggily hopped along, he came to a little place in the woods, all set around with green trees, and in the center was a large doll's tea table, all ready for a meal.

"Ha! This looks like an adventure already!" said the bunny uncle to himself. "And there's a party," he went on, as he saw the little girl named Alice, a March Hare (which is a sort of spring rabbit), a hatter man, with a very large hat, much larger than Uncle Wiggily's, on his head, and a dormouse. A dormouse (or doormouse) is one that crawls out under a door, you know, to get away from the cat.

"Oh, here's Uncle Wiggily!" cried Alice.

"Come right along and sit down. We didn't expect you!"

"Then if I'm unexpected, perhaps there isn't room for me," spoke Uncle Wiggily, looking at the March Hare.

"Oh, yes, there's plenty of room—more room than there is to eat," said the spring rabbit. "Besides, we really knew you were coming."

As this was just different from what Alice had said, Uncle Wiggily did not know what to believe.

"You see, it's the unexpected that always happens," went on the March Hare, "and, of course, being unexpected, you happened along, so we're glad to see you."

"Only there isn't anything to eat," said Alice. "You see, the Hatter's watch only keeps one kind of time—"

"That's what I do when I dance," interrupted Uncle Wiggily.

"We haven't come to that yet," Alice spoke gently. "But as the Hatter's watch only keeps tea-time we're always at the tea table, and the cake and tea were eaten long ago."

"And we always have to sit here, hoping the Hatter's watch will start off again, and bring us to breakfast or dinner on time," said the March Hare, who, Uncle Wiggily noticed, began to look rather mad and angry. "He's greased it with the best butter, but still his watch has stopped," the hare added.

"It's on account of the hard crumbs that got in the wheels," said the Hatter, dipping his watch in the cream pitcher. "I dare say they'll get soaked in time. But pass Uncle Wiggily the buns," he added, and Alice passed an empty plate which once had dog biscuits on, only Jackie and Peetie Bow Wow had eaten them all up—I should say down, for they swallowed them that way.

Uncle Wiggily was beginning to think this was a very queer tea party indeed, when, all of sudden, out from the bushes jumped a great, big, pink-striped Wabberjocky cat, who began singing:

"London Bridge is falling up,

On Yankee Doodle Dandy!

As we go 'round the mulberry bush

To buy a stick of candy."

"Well, what do you want?" asked the Mad March Hare of the Wabberjocky. "If you've come to wash the dishes you can't, for it's still tea time and it never will be anything else as long as he keeps dipping his watch in the molasses jug! That's what makes it so sticky-slow," and he tossed a tea biscuit at the Hatter, who caught it in his hat, just like a magician in the theater, and turned it into a lemon meringue pie.

"I've come for Uncle Wiggily!" cried the Wabberjocky. "I've come to take him off to my den, and then—"

Uncle Wiggily was just going to hide under the table, which he noticed was growing smaller and smaller, and he was wondering if it would be large enough to cover him, when—

All of a sudden the Mad March Hare caught up the bunny uncle's red, white and blue striped rheumatism crutch, and cried:

"You've come for Uncle Wiggily, have you? Well, we've no time for that!" and with this the March Hare smashed the crutch down on the Hatter's watch, "Bang!" breaking it all to pieces!

"There, I guess it'll go now!" cried the March Hare, and indeed the wheels of the watch went spinning while the spring suddenly uncurled, and one end, catching around Uncle Wiggily's left hind leg, flew out and tossed him safely away over the trees, until he fell down on his soft soldier tent, right in front of his own hollow stump bungalow. So he was saved from the Wabberjocky.

"Well! That was an adventure!" cried the bunny uncle. "I wonder what happened to the rest of them? I must find out." And if the laundry man doesn't let the plumber take the bath tub away for the gold fish to play tag in, I'll tell you next about Uncle Wiggily and the Cheshire Cat.

CHAPTER III

UNCLE WIGGILY AND THE CHESHIRE CAT

Uncle Wiggily Longears, the rabbit gentleman, was hopping along through the woods one day, wondering what sort of an adventure he would have, and he was thinking about Alice in Wonderland and what a queer tea party he had been to the day before, when the Mad March Hare smashed the Hatter's watch because the hands always stayed at 5 o'clock tea time.

"If anything like that is going to happen to me today," said the bunny uncle to himself, "I ought to have brought Nurse Jane Fuzzy Wuzzy along, so she could enjoy the fun. I'll just hop along and if anything queer starts I'll go back after her."

So he went on a little farther, and, all of a sudden, he saw, lying on the woodland path, a piece of cheese.

"Ha!" cried Uncle Wiggily. "I wonder if Jollie or Jillie Longtail, the mouse children, dropped that out of their trap? I'll take it to them, I guess."

He picked up the bit of cheese, thinking how glad the mousie boy and girl would be to have it back, when, all at once, he heard behind him a voice asking:

"Oh, did you find it? I'm so glad, thank you!" and from under a bush out stepped a cat wearing a large smile on the front of its face. The cat stretched out its claw and took the bit of cheese from Uncle Wiggily.

"Oh! Is that yours?" asked the bunny gentleman, in surprise.

"It's Cheshire cheese; isn't it?" asked the cat.

"I—I believe so," answered the bunny. "Yes," he added as he looked and made sure, "it is Cheshire cheese."

"Then, as I'm the Cheshire cat it's mine. Cheshire cat meet your cheese! Cheese, meet your cat! How do you do? So glad to see you!" and the cat shook paws with the cheese just as if Uncle Wiggily had introduced them.

"I dare say it's all right," went on the bunny uncle.

"Of course it is!" laughed the cat, smiling more than ever. "I'm so glad you found my cheese. I was afraid the March Hare had taken it for that silly 5 o'clock tea party. But I'm glad he didn't. At first I took you for the March Hare. You look like him, being a rabbit."

"My birthday is not in March, it is in April," said Uncle Wiggily, bowing.

"That's better," spoke the Cheshire cat. "You have done me a great favor by finding my cheese, and I hope to be able to do you one some day."

"Pray do not mention it," spoke the bunny uncle, modest-like and shy, as he always was. He was just going to ask about Alice in Wonderland when the cat ran away with the cheese.

"Never mind," thought Uncle Wiggily. "That was the beginning of an adventure, anyhow. I wonder what the next part will be?" He did not have long to wait.

All of a sudden, as he was walking along through the woods, sort of leaning on his red, white and blue striped barber pole rheumatism crutch, there was a rustling in the bushes and out popped a whole lot of hungry rats.

"Ah, there IT is!" cried one rat, seizing hold of Uncle Wiggily by his ears.

"Yes, and just in time, too!" cried another, grabbing the bunny by his paws. "Into our den with IT before the mouse trap comes along and takes IT away from us!"

With that the rats, of which there were about five hundred and sixteen, began hustling Uncle Wiggily down a hole in the ground, and the first he knew they had him inside a wooden room in an underground house and they locked the door, taking the key out.

"What does this mean?" cried the bunny uncle. "Why do you treat me this way?"

"Why, IT can speak!" cried several of the rats, in surprise.

"Of course I can!" cried Uncle Wiggily, his pink nose twinkling. "But why do you call me IT?"

"Because you are a piece of cheese," said one rat, "and we always call cheese IT."

"Cheese? I, cheese?" asked astonished Uncle Wiggily.

"Of course," cried the biggest rat of all. "You're Cheshire cheese. Why, you perfume the whole room! We're so hungry for you. We thought the grocer had forgotten to send you. But it's all right now. Oh, what a delightful meal we shall have. We love Cheshire cheese," and the rats in the room with Mr. Longears looked very hungrily at the bunny uncle – very hungrily indeed.

"Oh, what shall I do?" thought Uncle Wiggily. "I see what has happened. When I picked up the Cheshire cat's piece of Cheshire cheese some of the perfume from it must have stuck to my paws. The rats smelled that and think I'm it. IT!" murmured the bunny gentleman. "As if I were a game of tag! IT!"

The rats in the locked room were very busy, getting out their cheese knives and plates, and poor Uncle Wiggily hardly knew what to do with this most unpleasant adventure happening to him, when, all of a sudden, right in the middle of the room, there appeared a big, smiling mouth, with a cheerful grin spread all over it. Just a smile it was, and nothing more.

"Oh!" cried Uncle Wiggily in surprise. "Oh!"

With that all the rats looked up and, seeing the smile, one exclaimed:

"I smell a cat! Oh, woe is me! I smell a cat!"

Then, all of a sudden the smile grew larger and larger. Then a nose seemed to grow out of nothing, then some whiskers, then a pair of blazing eyes, and then ears – a head, legs, claws and a body, and finally there stood the Cheshire cat in the midst of the rats.

"Scat, rats," meaouwed the Cheshire cat. "Scat!"

"How did you get in here?" asked one rat.

"Yes, tell us!" ordered another. "How did you get in past the locked door?"

"Through the keyhole," said the Cheshire cat. "I sent my smile in first, and then it was easy for my body to follow. Now you scat and leave Uncle

Wiggily alone!" and with that the cat grinned larger than ever, showing such sharp teeth that the rats quickly unlocked the door and ran away, leaving the bunny uncle quite safe.

"Alice in Wonderland, most magically knew of the trouble you were in," said the Cheshire cat, "so she sent me to help you, which I was glad to do, as you had helped me. My Cheshire cheese, that you found for me when I had lost it, was very good!"

Then Uncle Wiggily hopped back to his bungalow, and the cat went to see Alice; and if the paper cutter doesn't slice the bread board all up into pieces of cake for the puppy dog's party, I'll tell you next about Uncle Wiggily and the Dormouse.

CHAPTER IV

UNCLE WIGGILY AND THE DORMOUSE

"Tap! Tap! Tap!" came a knock on the door of the hollow stump bungalow one morning. Uncle Wiggily Longears, the rabbit gentleman who lived in the woods, called out:

"Please come in!"

In hopped Dickie Chip-Chip, the sparrow boy postchap, with a letter for the bunny gentleman.

"Ha! That's nice!" explained Uncle Wiggily as he took the envelope. "I hope it's a valentine!"

"A valentine this time of year!" laughed Dickie. "This is June, Uncle Wiggily!"

"Oh, so it is. However, I'll read it." And when Dickie flew on to deliver the rest of his letters Uncle Wiggily read his own. It was very short, and said:

"If you want a new hat, come to the green meadow as soon as you read this."

"Ha! If I want a new hat!" thought the bunny uncle. "Well, I do need one. But who knew that I did? This is very strange and mysterious. Ha! I have it! This must be from Alice in Wonderland. She is giving me a little surprise."

So, telling Nurse Jane Fuzzy Wuzzy, his muskrat lady housekeeper, that he was going out to get a new hat, away hopped Uncle Wiggily, over the fields and through the woods until he came to the green meadow.

In the middle of the meadow was a little grove of trees, and half way there Uncle Wiggily heard a sad little voice saying:

"Oh, dear! What trouble I'm in!"

"Trouble!" cried the bunny gentleman twinkling his pink nose. "Ha! That sounds like old times! Let me help some one. But who is it?"

"It is I. The little Dormouse," was the answer, and, looking down, Uncle Wiggily saw the tiny creature who had been at the queer tea party when the Mad March Hare smashed the Hatter's 5 o'clock watch.

The tail of the poor little Dormouse was caught fast in between two stones and she could not move, but Uncle Wiggily quickly loosened it for her and she was very thankful to get out.

"I was afraid I'd be late," said the Dormouse. "I have to hurry on to help the Queen of Hearts put sugared cheese on the blackberry tarts for the King's birthday. I'll see you again, Uncle Wiggily."

"I hope so," spoke the bunny uncle, as he hurried away to get his new hat, all the while wondering whether or not he would see Alice from Wonderland.

Uncle Wiggily reached the green meadow trees, but no one else was there. He looked up and down, and all around, but there was not even an old hat in sight, to say nothing of a new one.

"I wonder if this letter is an April fool joke?" thought the bunny uncle, taking from his pocket the envelope Dickie had given him. "No, if it's the month of June it can't be April Fool's Day, any more than it can be time for valentines," said the bunny. "But I wonder where my hat is?"

Hardly had Uncle Wiggily said this, out loud, than, all of a sudden, a voice cried:

"Here's your hat!"

With that something seemed to drop down from the clouds, or maybe it was from one of the trees. But whatever it was it completely covered Uncle Wiggily out of sight. It was just as if you took a large bowl and turned it upside down over a grasshopper, only, of course, Uncle Wiggily was not a grasshopper, though he did jump around a lot.

And, at first, in the sudden darkness, the rabbit gentleman thought it was a bowl that, perhaps, the circus elephant's little boy had turned over on him just for fun.

Then, making his pink nose twinkle very fast, so that it shone in the dark like a firefly lantern, Uncle Wiggily was able to see that he was inside a large, tall, silk hat. When it had dropped over him it had shut out all the sunlight, making it quite dark inside where the bunny was.

"Yes, this is a hat!" said Uncle Wiggily to himself. "But what a funny way to give it to me! And it's so large! Instead of my new hat going outside my head, my head is inside the hat. This will never do! I must get out and see what the trouble is. This must be the elephant's hat, it's so large."

But when Uncle Wiggily tried to lift up one edge of the hat, to crawl out, he found he could not. Some one seemed to be sitting on top of the hat, which was shaped like the silk stovepipe one Uncle Wiggily always wore. And a voice cried:

"Hold it tight and he can't get out!"

"Oh, I'm holding it tight!" was the answer.

Then Uncle Wiggily knew what had happened. Some one had played a sad trick on him. And it was two bad old skillery-scalery alligators. They had borrowed the Wonderland Hatter's hat—which was very large. Nor had they told the Hatter what they wanted of it, for if they had he never would have let them borrow it to make trouble for Uncle Wiggily.

The alligators had climbed up the tree with the big hat, and, after sending Uncle Wiggily the note, they had waited until he came to the field. Then from the branches above they dropped the hat down over him and sat on it.

"And I can't get out!" cried Uncle Wiggily. "That's the worst of it! I can't get out, and those bad alligators will reach under and grab me and—"

"No they won't!" cried a little squeaky voice down low on the ground, just outside the hat.

"Why not?" asked Uncle Wiggily, hopeful like.

"Because I am the Dormouse whom you helped," was the answer. "Now, listen! With my sharp teeth I am going to cut a door in the side of the hat where the alligators, sitting up on top, can't see it. Then you can get out."

So the Dormouse, being made for just such work, as you can tell by its name, gnawed a door in the side of the Hatter's hat, and out crawled the bunny rabbit gentleman before the alligators could grab him. And the bunny and the Dormouse got safely away, Mr. Longears being very thankful, indeed, for having been helped by the little creature.

So the alligators had nothing for dinner but stewed pears, and if our dog doesn't leave his tail on the wrong side of the fence, so the cat can use it for a dusting brush, I'll tell you next about Uncle Wiggily and the Gryphon.

CHAPTER V

UNCLE WIGGILY AND THE GRYPHON

Uncle Wiggily Longears, the nice rabbit gentleman, had just finished shaving his whiskers in his hollow stump bungalow one morning when Nurse Jane Fuzzy Wuzzy, his muskrat lady housekeeper, came to his door, knocked gently by flapping her tail against it, and said:

"If you please, Mr. Longears, there's a young lady to see you."

"Of course I'm pleased," answered Uncle Wiggily. "I always like to see young ladies, especially if they have light, fluffy hair. Has this one that kind?"

"Very much so," answered Nurse Jane. "Here she is now," and with that in came a nice young lady, or, rather, a tall girl, with flaxen hair.

"I'm afraid you don't remember me," she said, as Uncle Wiggily wiped the soap lather off the end of his pink, twinkling nose, where it had splashed by mistake, making it look like part of a frosted chocolate cake.

"Oh, yes, I do remember you!" cried the bunny gentleman, in his most jolly voice. "You're Alice from Wonderland, and you were very kind to help me grow smaller that time the big mosquito got me into his cave and I swelled up from eating cake."

"Oh, I'm so glad you remember me!" laughed Alice, for it was indeed she. "I've come to ask you to do me a bit of a favor. I have to go see the Gryphon, and I thought maybe you'd come with me, for I'm afraid he'll be real cross to me."

"You have to go see the Gryphon?" exclaimed Uncle Wiggily. "Who in the world is he?"

"Oh, he's a funny animal who lives in the same story book with me," explained Alice. "He's something between a dragon, a lion, an elephant, a flying fish and an alligator."

"Whew!" whistled Uncle Wiggily. "He must be a curious creature!"

"He is," Alice said. "And sometimes he's very cross, especially if the wind blows his veil up."

"If the wind blows his veil up?" asked Uncle Wiggily. "In the first place, why does he wear a veil, and in the second place, why should he be angry if the wind blows it?"

"There isn't any first or second place about it," spoke Alice, "for you never can tell in which place the Gryphon will be found. But he wears a veil because he is so ugly that every one runs away when one sees him, and he doesn't like that. And, of course, he doesn't like the wind to blow up his veil so folks can see how he really looks."

"Ah, ha! I understand," remarked the bunny. "But if he is so cross why do you want to go to see him?"

"I don't want to," replied Alice, "but I have to, because it's that way in the book. You see, to make everything come out right, the Gryphon takes me to the Mock Turtle, who tells me a funny story, and so now I've come to see if you'll take me to the Gryphon?"

"I will," promised Uncle Wiggily, washing the soap lather out of his ears. "But where shall we find him?"

"Oh, that's the question!" laughed Alice, just as though Uncle Wiggily had asked a riddle. "You have three guesses," she went on.

The bunny gentleman twinkled his pink nose, so that he might think better, and then he said:

"I'll tell you what we'll do. We'll go for a walk, and make believe I'm looking for an adventure. Then I may find the Gryphon for you."

"Fine!" cried Alice, and, Uncle Wiggily having finished shaving, he and Alice set out together over the fields and through the wood, her hand holding the bunny's paw.

"Now we must keep a sharp watch for the Gryphon," said Alice, who had had so many adventures in Wonderland that it took a whole book to tell of them. "You never know whether he'll appear like an elephant, a dragon, a lion or a big bird, for he has wings," she said.

"Has he, indeed?" asked Uncle Wiggily. "Then I think I hear him coming now," he went on. "Listen, do you hear the buzzing?" And, surely enough, the air seemed filled with the buzzing and fluttering of wings. And then the sun appeared to be hidden by a cloud.

"That must be the Gryphon," said Uncle Wiggily.

Alice looked, and then she cried:

"Oh, no! It's a big cloud of bad, biting mosquitoes. It is the buzzing of their wings we hear! Oh, Uncle Wiggily, you haven't your talcum powder bean-shooter gun with you, and here come a billion-million mosquitoes!"

"That's right!" cried the bunny uncle, as he, too, saw them. "We must hide or they will bite even our shoes off!"

So he and Alice looked for a place to hide, but there was none, and the buzzing mosquitoes cried:

"Ah, ha! Now we have that Uncle Wiggily Longears rabbit. He can't get away now, for he isn't a soldier today! And we'll get Alice from Wonderland, too!"

Well, the mosquitoes were just going to grab the bunny gentleman, and the nice little young lady girl, with the fluffy flaxen hair, when a voice out of the air cried:

"Oh, ho! No you're not going to get them, either!"

"Who says we are not?" asked the captain mosquito.

"I do!"

"And who are you?"

"I am the Gryphon!" was the answer. "And I have on my mosquito net veil. I'll catch all you bad biting bugs in my net, just as a professor catches butterflies. Whoop! Swoop! Here I come!"

And with that the Gryphon, raising his veil, which hung down from his big ears as from around a lady's big hat, made a net of it and, flying around, soon caught all the mosquitoes that would have bitten Uncle Wiggily and Alice.

And the mosquitoes that were not caught were so frightened at the fierce look on the Gryphon's face that they fainted, and couldn't bite even as much as a spoonful of mustard.

So the Gryphon drove the mosquitoes away and then he took Alice to see the Mock Turtle, while Uncle Wiggily hopped on home to his bungalow. And if the rubber doll doesn't bounce off the clothes horse when she rides to the candy store for some cornstarch pudding, I'll tell you next about Uncle Wiggily and the blue caterpillar.

CHAPTER VI

UNCLE WIGGILY AND THE CATERPILLAR

"Uncle Wiggily! Oh, Uncle Wiggily!" called Alice from Wonderland as she stood one day just outside the hollow stump bungalow where the rabbit gentleman had just finished his breakfast of carrot oatmeal with parsnip sauce sprinkled over the top.

"Do you want to come for another walk with me?" asked Alice as she ran up the bungalow front steps.

"Are you going to have the Gryphon take you to the Mock Turtle again?" the bunny gentleman wanted to know. "If you are, I'll bring my talcum powder gun along this time, to keep away the mosquitoes."

"No. I don't have to see the Gryphon today," replied Wonderland Alice with a laugh. "But the Duchess has sent me to find the Blue Caterpillar."

"The Duchess has sent you to find the Blue Caterpillar?" questioned Uncle Wiggily, wondering if he had heard rightly. "But who is the Duchess?"

"Oh, she's some relation to the Queen of Hearts," Alice answered. "She's in the book with me, the Duchess is. In the book-picture she always has a lot of trimming on her big hat, and she doesn't care whether or not she holds the baby upside down."

"Oh, yes, now I remember," Uncle Wiggily said, laughing as he thought of the baby. "And now about the Blue Caterpillar?"

"Oh, he's a sort of long, fuzzy bug, who sits on a toadstool smoking a pipe," explained Alice. "The Duchess wants him to come and smoke some hams for her."

"Smoke hams!" cried the bunny rabbit. "Why the very idonical idea! I've heard of men smoking tobacco — but hams — "

"Oh, you don't smoke hams in a pipe," said Alice with a laugh. "They take a ham before it is cooked, and hang it up in a cloud of smoke, or blow smoke on it, or do something to it with smoke, so it will dry and keep longer."

"What do they want to keep it for?" asked Uncle Wiggily. "I thought ham was to eat, with eggs."

"Oh, dear!" laughed Alice. "I wish you wouldn't ask me so many questions. You're like the Dormouse, or the Cheshire Cheese Cat or the Hatter. They were always asking the curiousestest questions like 'Who threw stones at the cherry tree?' or 'How did the soft egg get inside the hard shell without cracking it?' All things like that. I can't answer them!"

"Very well," said Uncle Wiggily, smiling at Alice. "I'll not ask you any more questions. Come on! We'll go find the Blue Caterpillar."

So off they started, the bunny rabbit gentleman and Wonderland Alice who had a day's vacation from the book with her name on it. Now and then she could slip out of the book covers and go off to have a real adventure with Uncle Wiggily.

The bunny uncle and the little girl with the pretty, flaxen hair had not gone very far over the fields and through the woods before, all of a sudden, as they were walking under some trees, something long and twisty and rubbery, like a big fire hose, reached out and grabbed them.

"Oh, my!" cried Alice, trying to get loose, which she could not do. "A big snake has us!"

"No," said Uncle Wiggily, looking around as best he could, for he, too, was held fast as was Alice. "This isn't a snake."

"What is it?" asked Alice.

"It's a bad circus elephant," said the bunny, "and he has caught us in his trunk. Oh, dear! Please let us go!" he begged the big animal.

"No," sadly answered the circus elephant, for it was indeed he. "I can't let you go, for if I do they will all sit on my back and bite me."

"Who will?" asked Uncle Wiggily, curious like.

"The mosquitoes," was the answer. "You see they have tried in so many ways to catch you, and haven't done it, Uncle Wiggily, that they finally came to me. About a million billion of them swarmed around me, and they said they'd bite me until I had the shiv-ivers if I did not help them catch you. So I had to promise that I would, though I did not want to, for I like you, Uncle Wiggily.

"If I hadn't promised, though, the mosquitoes would have bitten me, and though I seem to have a very thick skin I am very tender, not to say ticklish, when it comes to mosquito bites. So I hid here to catch you, and I'll have to hold you until the mosquitoes come to get you. I'm very sorry!" and the elephant wound his rubbery nose of a trunk still more tightly around Uncle Wiggily and Alice.

"Oh, dear!" said Alice. "What shall we do?"

"I don't know, I'm sure," answered the bunny. "This is quite too bad. If only the Blue Caterpillar—"

"Hush!" exclaimed a fuzzy voice down in the grass near the elephant's left front foot. "Don't say a word. I'll help you," and along came crawling a big Blue Caterpillar, with a folded toadstool umbrella and a long-stemmed pipe on his back.

"That elephant is very ticklish," said the Blue Caterpillar. "Watch me make him squirm. And when he squirms he'll have to uncurl his trunk to scratch himself, and when he does that—"

"We'll get away!" whispered Uncle Wiggily.

"Exactly!" said the Blue Caterpillar. So he crawled up the elephant's leg, and tickled the big animal on its ear.

"Oh, dear!" cried the elephant. "How itchy I am!" and he uncurled his trunk to scratch himself, and then Uncle Wiggily and Alice could run away safely, and the mosquitoes didn't get them after all. Then Alice told the Blue Caterpillar about the Duchess wanting the hams smoked and the crawling creature said he'd attend to it, and puff smoke on them from his pipe.

So everything came out all right, I'm glad to say, and if the starch doesn't all come out of the collar so it has to lie down instead of standing up straight at the moving picture show, I'll tell you next about Uncle Wiggily and the Hatter.

CHAPTER VII
UNCLE WIGGILY AND THE HATTER

"Oh, Uncle Wiggily!" called Nurse Jane Fuzzy Wuzzy, the muskrat lady housekeeper, as Mr. Longears, the rabbit gentleman, started to hop out of his hollow stump bungalow one morning. "Oh, Uncle Wiggily!"

"Well, what is it?" asked the bunny with a polite bow. "Do you want anything from the store?"

"Some carrot coffee, if you please," answered the muskrat lady. "When you finish your walk, and have had a nice adventure, bring home some coffee."

"I'll do it," promised Uncle Wiggily, and then, as he hopped along, over the fields and through the woods, he thought perhaps he had better buy the carrot coffee first.

"For," said he to himself, "I might have such a funny adventure that I'd forget all about what Nurse Jane told me."

Now you just wait and see what happens, if you please.

It did not take the bunny long to get the coffee; the monkey doodle gentleman who kept the store wrapping it up for him in a paper that had been twisted around a lollypop candy.

"It's a bit sticky and sweet," said the monkey doodle store keeper, speaking of the lollypop paper, "but that will stop the coffee from falling out."

"Fine!" laughed Uncle Wiggily, and then he hopped on to look for an adventure. He had not gone very far before when, all of a sudden, he heard a voice saying:

"Well, I don't know what to do about it, that's all! I never saw such trouble! The idea of wanting me to get ready for it this time of day!"

"Ha! Trouble!" thought Uncle Wiggily. "This is where I come in. What is it you can't get ready for this time of day, and who are you?" asked the bunny, for he saw no one.

"Oh, it's you, is it?" called a voice, and out from under a mulberry bush stepped a little man, with such a large hat that it covered him from head to foot.

"Oh, excuse me," said Uncle Wiggily. "You are—"

"The Hatter! Exactly! You have guessed it," said the little man, opening a window which was cut in the side of his hat. The window was just opposite his face, which was inside, so he could look out at the bunny gentleman.

"I'm the Hatter, from 'Alice in Wonderland,'" went on the little man. The bunny hadn't quite really guessed it, though he might if he had had time.

"And what is the trouble?" asked Uncle Wiggily.

"Oh, I've just been ordered by the Queen of Hearts to get up a tea party right away for Alice, who is expected any minute," went on the Hatter. "And here it is 10 o'clock in the morning, and the tea's at 5, and I haven't even started."

"You have lots of time," said Uncle Wiggily. "Hours and hours."

"Yes, but I haven't the tea!" cried the Hatter. "Don't mind me, but I'm as mad — as mad as — as lollypops, and there's nothing madder than them!" he said, sort of grinding his teeth. This grinding made Uncle Wiggily think of the coffee in his pocket. So, holding out the package, he said:

"I don't s'pose this would do, would it?"

"What?" asked the Hatter.

"It's coffee," went on the bunny, "but —"

"The very thing!" cried the Hatter, who was now smiling. "It will be just the thing for the 5 o'clock tea. We'll have it right here — I'll set the table," and opening two little doors lower down in his big hat, he stuck his arms through them and began brushing off a broad, flat stump near Uncle Wiggily.

"The stump will do for a table," said the Hatter. "This is great, Uncle Wiggily! We'll have tea for Alice after all, and make things happen as they do in the book. Don't mind me saying I was as mad as lollypops. I have to be mad — make believe, you know — or things won't come out right."

"I see," said Uncle Wiggily, remembering that it was quite stylish to be "as mad as a hatter," though he never before knew what it meant. "But you see, my dear sir," the rabbit went on, "I have only coffee to give you, and not tea."

"It doesn't matter," said the Hatter. "I'll boil it in a cocoanut shell, and it will do her very well," and with that he took out, from somewhere inside his hat, half a cocoanut shell. This he set on top of the stump on a little three-legged stool, and built a fire under it.

"But you need water to make coffee — I mean tea," said Uncle Wiggily.

"I have it!" cried the Hatter, and, picking up an umbrella plant growing near by, he squeezed some water from it into the cocoanut shell kettle.

Uncle Wiggily poured some of the ground coffee into the cocoanut shell of umbrella water, which was now boiling, and then the bunny exclaimed:

"But we have no sugar!"

"We'll sweeten it with the paper that came off the lollypop," said the Hatter, tearing off a bit of it and tossing it into the tea-coffee.

"What about milk?" asked Uncle Wiggily. "Alice may want cream in her coffee—I mean tea."

"Here we are!" cried the Hatter.

With that he picked a leaf from a milkweed plant growing near the flat stump and from that he squeezed out some drops of milk into a cup he made from a Jack-in-the-pulpit flower.

"Now we're all ready for 5 o'clock tea!" cried the Hatter, and just then along came Alice from Wonderland, with the March Hare, and they sat down to the stump table with Uncle Wiggily, who happened to have a piece of cherry pie in his pocket, so they had a nice little lunch after all. And the carrot coffee with milkweed cream in it, tasted like catnip tea, so everything came out all right.

And if the white shoes don't go down in the coal bin to play with the fire shovel and freeze their toes so they can't parade on the Board Walk, I'll tell you next about Uncle Wiggily and the Duchess.

CHAPTER VIII
UNCLE WIGGILY AND THE DUCHESS

Uncle Wiggily Longears, the rabbit gentleman, was hopping along through the woods one day, looking for an adventure, when, all of a sudden, he came to a door standing up between two trees. It was a regular door, with a knob, hinges and all, but the funny part of it was there didn't seem to be a room on either side of it.

"This is remarkable!" exclaimed Wiggily, "remarkable" meaning the same thing as queer. "It is very odd! Here is a door and the jamb—"

"Where's the jamb?" asked a little katydid, who was sitting on a leaf in the sun. "I'm very fond of jam."

"I didn't say j-a-m—the kind you eat on bread," spoke Uncle Wiggily. "I was talking about the j-a-m-b—with a b—"

"Bees make honey," said the katydid, "and honey's almost as good as jam. I'm not so fussy as all that. Jam or honey—honey or jam, it's all the same to me."

"No, there isn't any honey, either," said the bunny. "The jamb of the door is the wooden frame that goes around it, to hold it in place."

"Then I don't want any door jamb—I want bread and jam," said the katydid, hopping off to find her sister, Katydidn't, leaving Uncle Wiggily to stare at the lone door.

"Well," said the rabbit gentleman to himself, "I may as well see what's on the other side. Though a door standing all by itself in the woods is the strangest thing I've ever seen."

However, he turned the knob, opened the door and stepped through, and, to his surprise, he found himself in a big kitchen which seemed magically to have appeared the moment he entered the very surprising place. At one end was a big stove, with a hot fire in it, and on the stove was a boiling kettle of soup, which was being stirred by a big fat cook lady, who was shaped like a ham, without the string in the end, of course. For the cook could stand up and didn't need to be hung on a nail as a ham is hung before it's cooked.

In front of the fire was another large lady with a bonnet on almost as big as the Hatter's hat. Over the bonnet was a fluffy, flowing veil.

"Now please be quiet—do!" exclaimed the sitting down lady to something in her lap, and Uncle Wiggily saw that it was a baby. "Come, cook!" she cried. "Is that hot soup ready yet for the baby?"

"Not yet, mum. But it soon will be," answered the cook, and Uncle Wiggily was just going to say something about not giving a little baby hot soup, when the door opened again, and in came Alice from Wonderland.

"Oh, I'm so glad you're here, Uncle Wiggily!" cried Alice. "Now it will be all right."

"What will?" asked the bunny. "What will be right?"

"My left shoe," said Alice. "You see I just came from the Pool of Tears, and everything got all mixed up. When I came out I had two left shoes instead of one being a right, but now you are here it's all right—I mean one is right and the other is left, as it should be," and with that Alice put on one shoe she had been carrying in her hand, and smiled.

"But who is this?" asked Uncle Wiggily, pointing with his red, white and blue striped rheumatism crutch at the big lady holding the baby, which was now squirming like an angle worm.

"It's the Duchess—a friend of the Queen of Hearts," answered Alice. "I'll introduce you to her in a minute. Are you fond of sneezing?"

"Only when I have a cold," answered Uncle Wiggily. "Why do you ask?" and he began to think he was having a very funny adventure indeed. "Why should I be fond of sneezing?"

"Because you'll have to whether you like it or not," answered Alice. "The Duchess is going to talcum powder the baby now—it's just had a bath."

With that the duchess, who is the wife of a duke, you know, called:

"Here, cook! Never mind the soup. Give me the pepper!"

"Goodness me sakes alive and some horseradish lollypops!" cried Uncle Wiggily. "She isn't going to talcum powder the baby with pepper, is she?"

"Of course," answered Alice. "It's that way in the book from which I came to have an adventure with you, so, of course, pepper it has to be. Look out—here come the sneezes!" and Alice got out her handkerchief.

Uncle Wiggily saw the duchess, with a funny smile on her big face, take the pepper-box the cook gave her and start to sprinkle the black stuff over the baby in her lap. The baby was cooing and gurgling—as all babies do after their bath—and didn't seem at all to mind her being peppered.

"They season chickens and turkeys with salt and pepper, so why not babies?" asked Alice of Uncle Wiggily. The bunny gentleman was just going to say he did not know the answer to that riddle, when the door suddenly opened again and in came a great big dodo bird, which is something like a skillery-scalery alligator, only worse, with a beak like that of a mosquito.

"Ah, ha!" chirped the dodo. "At last I have found him!" and he made a dart with his big beak for Uncle Wiggily. The dodo was just going to grab the bunny gentleman in his claws, and Mr. Longears was so shivery he didn't know what to do, when the duchess, suddenly tossing the baby to the cook, cried:

"Ha! No you don't! I guess it's you I want to pepper instead!" and with that she shook the box of pepper at the dodo, who began sneezing as hard as he could sneeze.

"Aker-choo! Aker-choo! Aker-choo!" sneezed the dodo.

"Keer-zoo! Keer-zoo! Keer-zoo!" sneezed the duchess.

"Goo-snitzio! Goo-snitzio! Goo-snitzio!" sneezed Alice.

"Fizz-buzzy-wuzz! Fizz-buzzy-wuzz! Fizz-buzzy-wuzz!" sneezed Uncle Wiggily, and then the dodo himself gave another very large special five and ten cent store sale sneeze and blew himself backward out of the door. So he didn't get Uncle Wiggily after all.

"And now we are all right," said Alice, when they had all finished sneezing, including the baby. "Have some soup, Uncle Wiggily."

So the bunny did, finding it very good, and made from cabbage and pretzels and then he went home to his stump bungalow.

And if the lollypop stick doesn't have to go out and help the wash lady hold up the clothesline when it goes fishing for apple pie I'll tell you next about Uncle Wiggily and the cook.

CHAPTER IX

UNCLE WIGGILY AND THE COOK

"Well, Mr. Longears, I shall have to leave you all alone today," said Nurse Jane Fuzzy Wuzzy, the muskrat lady housekeeper, as she gave Uncle Wiggily, the bunny rabbit gentleman, his breakfast in the hollow stump bungalow one morning.

"Leave me all alone—how does that happen?" asked Uncle Wiggily, sort of sad and sorrowful like. "Do you mean you are going to leave me for good?"

"Oh, no; I'm just going to be busy all day sewing mosquito shirts for the animal boy soldiers who are going off to war. Since you taught them how to shoot their talcum powder guns at the bad biting bugs, Sammie Littletail, your rabbit nephew, and Johnnie and Billie Bushytail, the squirrels; Jackie and Peetie Bow Wow, the puppy dogs, and all the other Woodland chaps have been bothered with the mosquitoes."

"They made war enough on me," said Uncle Wiggily.

"And, since they could not catch you, they are starting war against your friends," went on Nurse Jane, "so I am making mosquito shirts for the animal boys. I'll be away sewing all day, and you'll have to get your own lunch, I'm afraid."

"I'm not afraid!" laughed brave Uncle Wiggily. "If I could get away from the bad, biting mosquitoes, I guess I can get my own lunch. Besides, maybe Alice from Wonderland will come along and help me."

"Maybe," spoke Nurse Jane. Then the muskrat lady, tying her tail up in a pink-blue hair ribbon, scurried off, while Uncle Wiggily hopped over the fields and through the woods, looking for an adventure.

But adventures, or things that happen to you, seemed to be scarce that day, and it was noontime before the bunny gentleman hardly knew it.

"Well!" he exclaimed. "I'm getting hungry, and, as I didn't bring any cherry pie with me I'll have to skip along to my hollow stump bungalow for something to eat."

Nurse Jane had left some things on the table for the bunny gentleman to eat for his lunch. There were cold carrot sandwiches, cold cabbage tarts, cold turnip unsidedowns — which are like turnovers only different — and cold lettuce pancakes.

"But it seems to me," said Uncle Wiggily, "it seems to me that I would like something hot. I think I'll make a soup of all these things as I saw the cook doing when I went through the funny little door and met Alice from Wonderland in the kitchen of the Duchess."

So, getting a large soup kettle, Uncle Wiggily put into it the cold carrot sandwiches, the cold lettuce pancakes, the cold cabbage tarts and so on. Then he built a fire in the stove.

"For," said he, "if those things are good cold they are better hot. I shall have a fine hot lunch."

Then Uncle Wiggily sat down to wait for the things to cook, and every once in a while he would look at the kettle on the stove and say:

"Yes, I shall have a fine, hot lunch!"

And then, all of a sudden, after the bunny rabbit gentleman had said this about five-and-ten-cent-store times a voice cried:

"Indeed you will have a hot lunch!" and all of a sudden into the kitchen of the hollow stump bungalow came the red hot flamingo bird, eager to burn the rabbit gentleman.

"Oh!" exclaimed Uncle Wiggily. "I — I don't seem to know you very well."

"You'll know me better after a bit," said the red flamingo bird, clashing its beak like a pair of tailor's shears. "I'm the bird that Alice from Wonderland used for a croquet mallet when she played with the Queen of Hearts."

"Oh, now I know!" said the bunny. "Won't you have lunch with me?" he asked, trying to be polite. "I'm having a hot lunch, though Nurse Jane left me a cold one, and — "

"You are going to have a much hotter lunch than you imagine!" said the red flamingo bird. "Look out! I'm getting sizzling hot!" And indeed he was, which made him such a red color, I suppose. "I'm going to burn you!" cried the bird to Uncle Wiggily, sticking out his red tongue.

"Burn me? Why?" asked the poor bunny gentleman.

"Oh, because I have to burn somebody, and it might as well be you!" said the flamingo. "Look out, now!"

"Ha! Indeed! And it's you who had better look out!" cried a new voice. And with that the cook — the same big lady, shaped like a ham, whom Uncle Wiggily had last seen in the kitchen of the Duchess — this cook hopped nimbly in through a window of the hollow stump bungalow.

"I'll fix him!" she cried, catching up the flatirons from the shelf over the stove and throwing them at the flamingo. "Get out! Scat! Sush! Run away!" And she threw the fire shovel, the dustpan, the sink shovel, the stove lifter, the broom and the coal scuttle at the flamingo. My, but that cook was a thrower!

She didn't hit the red flamingo bird with any of the things she threw, but she tossed them so very hard, and seemingly with such anger, that the bird was frightened.

"This is no place for me!" cried the flaming red bird, drawing in his red tongue. "I'll go make it hot for Mr. Whitewash, the polar bear. He might like some heat for a change from his cake of ice."

Then the red flamingo bird, not burning Uncle Wiggily at all, flew away, and the cook, after she had picked up all the kitchen things she had thrown, came in and had a hot lunch with Uncle Wiggily, who thanked her very much.

"I'm glad you came," said the bunny, "but I didn't know you cooks threw things."

"Oh, I'm from the Wonderland Alice book, which makes me different," the cook answered. And she was queer. But everything came out all right, you see, and if the trolley car conductor doesn't punch the transfer so hard that it falls off the seat, I'll tell you next about Uncle Wiggily and the Baby.

CHAPTER X

UNCLE WIGGILY AND THE BABY

"Well," said Uncle Wiggily Longears, the rabbit gentleman, to himself, as he stood in the middle of the woods and looked around. "I don't seem to be going to have any adventures today at all. I wonder what's the matter?"

Something was wrong, that is certain.

The bunny uncle had been hopping along all the morning, and part of the afternoon, and not a single adventure had he found. Almost always something happened to him, but this time was different.

He had not met Alice from Wonderland, nor any of her queer relations, and Uncle Wiggily had not seen any of his animal boy or girl friends, so the rabbit gentleman was beginning to feel a bit lonesome.

Then, all of a sudden, before you could count a million (providing you had time and wanted to), Uncle Wiggily saw, fluttering from a tree, what he thought was a flag.

"That's queer," he said to himself, only out loud. "I wonder if any of my mosquito enemies have made a camp there under the trees, and are flying the flag before they come to bite me? I'll go closer and see."

Uncle Wiggily was very brave, you know, even if he only had his red, white and blue striped rheumatism crutch instead of the talcum powder popgun that shot bean-bag bullets. So up he went to where he thought he saw the mosquito enemy's flag fluttering, and my goodness me sakes alive and some chocolate cake ginger snaps! It wasn't the mosquito flag at all, which shows that we ought never to be afraid until we are sure what a thing is — and sometimes not then.

"Why, it's a lady's veil!" cried Uncle Wiggily, as he looked at the fluttering thing. And, as he said that, someone, who was sitting on an old log, turned around, and — there was the Wonderland Duchess herself — the queer, stout lady who looked like a barrel of flour — very rich you know!

"Oh, hello, Uncle Wiggily!" called the Duchess, who is a sort of princess grown up. "I'm glad to see you. I have a friend of yours here with me!"

"Do you mean Alice?" asked the bunny.

"No, this time it's the Baby," answered the Duchess, and then Uncle Wiggily saw that she had a live baby in her arms upside down. I mean the baby was upside down, not the arms of the Duchess, though perhaps it would have been better that way.

"Bless me!" cried Uncle Wiggily. "That's no way to hold the child."

"Oh, indeed!" said the Duchess, sort of sniffing proud like. "Then if you know so much about holding babies, take this one. I have to go make a rice pudding," and before Uncle Wiggily could stop her she tossed the baby to him as if it were a ball and ran away, crying:

"Rice! Rice! Who has the rice pudding?"

"Oh, my!" Uncle Wiggily started to say, but that was all he had time for, as he had to catch Baby, which he managed to do right side up. This was a good thing, I think.

"You poor little dear!" cried the bunny uncle as he smoothed out the Baby's clothes and looked around for a nursing bottle or a rattle box. And, as he was doing this, and while the Baby was trying to close its lips, which it had opened to cry with when it found itself skedaddling through the air — while this was going on, some one gave a loud laugh, and Uncle Wiggily, looking around in surprise, saw Alice from Wonderland.

"Well!" said the bunny. "I'm glad to see you, but what is there to laugh at?"

"The — the baby!" said Alice, sort of choking like, for she was trying to talk and laugh at the same time.

"Why should you laugh at a poor baby, whom no one seems to know how to care for?" asked Uncle Wiggily. "Why, I ask you?"

"Oh! But look what it's turning into!" said Alice, pointing.

The bunny uncle looked at what he held in his paws. It was wiggling, twisting and squirming in such a funny way, squee-geeing its dress all up around its face that for a moment Uncle Wiggily could not get a good look, but, when he did, he cried:

"My goodness me sakes alive and some bacon gravy! It's a little pig!"

And so it was! As he held it the baby had turned into a tiny pig, with a funny nose and half-shut eyes.

"Bless my rheumatism crutch!" cried Uncle Wiggily. "What made it do that?"

"Because it's that way in the book where I came from," said Alice. "You read and you'll see that the baby which the Duchess gives me to hold turns into a little pig."

"But she gave it to ME to hold!" cried Uncle Wiggily.

"It's much the same thing," spoke Alice. "As long as it's a pig it doesn't matter."

"But dear me hum suz dud!" cried the bunny. "I don't want to be carrying around a little pig. Of course I like pigs, and I'm very fond of my friends Curley and Floppy Twisty-tail, the little grunters. But this baby pig—"

And, just as Uncle Wiggily said that, who should come along but a bad old skillery-scalery hump-tailed alligator, walking on his hind legs, with his two front claws stretched out in front of him.

"Ah, ha!" cried the bad alligator, who had promised to be good, but who had not kept his word. "Ah, ha! At last I have caught you, Uncle Wiggily, and Wonderland Alice, too!"

He was just going to grab them when the little Baby Pig, who had been squirming very hard all the while, finally squirmed out of Uncle Wiggily's paws, fell to the ground, and then, running right between the legs of the alligator, as pigs always do run, the squealing chap upset the bad, unpleasant creature, knocking him over in a frontward somersault and also backward peppersault down the steps.

"Oh, my goodness!" cried the skillery-scalery alligator. "I'm killed!" Which he wasn't at all, but he thought so, and this frightened him so much that he ran away and didn't catch Uncle Wiggily or Alice after all, for which I'm glad.

And if the puppy dog doesn't take all the bark off the sassafras tree and leave none for the pussy cat to polish her claws on, I'll tell you next about Uncle Wiggily and the Mock-Turtle.

CHAPTER XI

UNCLE WIGGILY AND THE MOCK-TURTLE

"Oh, Uncle Wiggily! Will you please take me with you this morning?" asked a little voice, somewhere down near the lower, or floor-end, of the old rabbit gentleman's rheumatism crutch, as Mr. Longears sat at the breakfast table in his hollow stump bungalow. "Please take me with you!"

"Well, who are you, and where do you want to be taken?" asked the bunny.

"Oh, I'm Squeaky-Eeky, the little cousin mouse," was the answer, "and I want you to take me with you on one of your walks, so I can have an adventure as you do with Alice in Wonderland."

"But perhaps I may not see Alice in Wonderland," spoke Uncle Wiggily. "I do not always have that pleasure."

"Well, then, perhaps we'll see the Baby or the Duchess, or the Gryphon or some of the funny folk who make such jolly fun with you," went on Squeaky-Eeky. "I have a holiday from school today, because they are painting the blackboards white, and I'd like to come with you."

"Come along then!" cried Uncle Wiggily, giving the little cousin mouse a bit of cheese cake with some lettuce sugar sprinkled over the top. "We'll see what sort of adventure happens today."

So, calling good-bye to Nurse Jane Fuzzy Wuzzy, the muskrat lady housekeeper, Uncle Wiggily and Squeaky-Eeky started off over the fields and through the woods. They had not gone very far before, all at once, as they walked along a little path under the trees they saw a funny thing lying near a clump of ferns.

It looked like a mud turtle at first, but after peering at it through his glasses Uncle Wiggily saw that the larger part was made of a half-round stone. In front of that was part of a broken rubber ball, and sticking out at the four corner places were four pieces of wood, like little claws, while at the back was a piece of an old leather boot.

"My! I wonder what in the world this can be?" said Uncle Wiggily, surprised like.

"Maybe it's something from Alice in Wonderland," spoke Squeaky-Eeky, the cousin mouse.

"You are right—I am!" exclaimed a voice. "I am the Mock-Turtle and I have just gotten out of the soup."

"Oh, I'm so glad to meet you!" cried Squeaky. "I've always wanted to see what a real mock turtle looked like, ever since I read the book about Alice."

"Hum!" grunted the queer creature. "There's no such thing as a real mock turtle any more than there is a make-believe toothache."

"I hope you never have that," said Squeaky-Eeky, politely.

"Thank you, I don't care for any," answered the Mock-Turtle, just as if the little cousin mouse had passed the cakes. And then the turtle began to sing:

"Speak gently to your toothache drops,

And do not let them fall.

And when you have the measle-mumps,

They'll scarcely hurt at all."

"Mine did," said Squeaky-Eeky, wondering if this was what Alice would have answered. But the Mock-Turtle kept right on with:

"Once a tramp was seated on

A chair made out of cheese.

He ate the legs and then he fell

Down with a terrible sneeze."

"That isn't right," said Squeaky-Eeky. "It's a trap that was baited with a piece of cheese, and—"

"Hush!" suddenly exclaimed the Mock-Turtle. "Here he comes!"

"Who?" asked the little cousin mouse. "Do you mean the tramp?"

Before the Mock-Turtle could answer along came shuffling a big, shaggy bear. At first Uncle Wiggily and the little cousin mouse thought perhaps it was Neddie or Beckie Stubtail, one of the good bear children, but instead it was a bad old tramp sort of a bear — the kind that goes about taking honey out of beehives.

"Ah, ha!" growled the bear. "A rabbit and a mouse! That's fine for me! I shall have a good dinner, I'm sure!" and he smacked his red tongue against his teeth.

"Where will you get your dinner?" asked Uncle Wiggily, curious like.

"There is no restaurant or kitchen around here," went on Squeaky-Eeky.

"Never you mind about that!" cried the bear. "I'll attend to you at dessert. Just now I want Uncle Wiggily to come here and count how many teeth I have," and he opened his mouth real wide, the bear did.

"Oh, but I don't want to count your teeth," said the poor bunny gentleman, for well he knew what the bear's trick would be. The bear wanted to bite Uncle Wiggily.

"You must count my teeth!" growled the shaggy creature, coming close to Uncle Wiggily.

"No, let me do it!" suddenly cried the Mock-Turtle. "I am good at counting."

"Well, it doesn't make any difference who does it," said the bear. Then, going close over to where the Mock-Turtle sat on the path, the bear opened wide his mouth. And then, just as he would have done to the rabbit gentleman, the bear made a savage bite for the Mock-Turtle.

But you know what happened. Instead of biting on something good, like a lollypop, the bear bit on the hard stone, of which the top part of Mock, or Make-Believe, Turtle was made, and the stone was so gritty and tough that the bear's teeth all broke off, and then he couldn't bite even a jelly fish.

"Oh, wow! Oh, woe is me!" cried the bear, as he ran to see if he could find a dentist to make him some false teeth.

"And he didn't hurt me a bit," laughed the Mock-Turtle, made of stone, wood and leather, who was built that way on purpose to fool bad bears and such like. "I don't mind in the least being bitten," said the pretend turtle.

"But you saved my life, and Squeaky-Eeky's, too," said Uncle Wiggily. "I thank you!" Then the Mock-Turtle crawled away and the bunny and mousie girl had a fine time together. And if the milk wagon doesn't go swimming down on the board walk with the watering cart and make the ice cream jump over the lollypop, I'll tell you next about Uncle Wiggily and the Lobster.

CHAPTER XII

UNCLE WIGGILY AND THE LOBSTER

"You'll be home to supper, won't you?" asked Nurse Jane Fuzzy Wuzzy, the muskrat lady housekeeper, as she saw her friend, Uncle Wiggily Longears, the rabbit gentleman, hopping down off the front porch of the hollow stump bungalow one morning.

"Oh, yes, I'll be home," he answered, "I'm just going to look for a little adventure."

Then, not having been on the board walk in quite a while, Uncle Wiggily went down to the ocean seashore beach.

"For," said the old rabbit gentleman to himself, "I have not had a seashore adventure in some time. And, perhaps, my friend, Alice, from Wonderland, may be down there. I know in her story book there are many curious things that happen near the sea."

So down to the shore went Uncle Wiggily and as he was walking along, looking at the funny marks his feet made in the wet sand, all of a sudden he came to a pile of damp, green seaweed, and from underneath it he heard a voice calling:

"Oh, help me out! Please help me out!"

"Ha! That sounds like some one in trouble!" Uncle Wiggily said. "I must help them." Then with his red, white and blue striped rheumatism crutch that Nurse Jane had gnawed for him out of a lollypop stick, the bunny poked away the seaweed, and underneath it, all tangled up so he could hardly move, was a Lobster gentleman.

"Oh, it was so good of you to get me out," said the Lobster as he gave a flip-flap with his tail. "An old crab, who doesn't like me, piled the seaweed over my back as I was taking a nap in the sun. My long thin legs were all tangled in it, and even with my big pinching claws I could not get loose, and I was so afraid I'd be late."

"Late for what?" asked Uncle Wiggily, wondering where the Lobster was going.

"To the dance—the quadrille, of course," was the answer.

"Oh, now I remember," said the bunny. "It's in the Wonderland Alice book. You have to go to a dance, don't you?"

"Exactly," said the Lobster. "I'd be pleased to have you come with me."

"I will," promised Uncle Wiggily, thinking maybe he would have an adventure there. So down the beach started the Lobster gentleman and the bunny uncle. On and on they went for a long, long time, it seemed to Uncle Wiggily, and it was getting quite late, as he could tell by the star fish which were twinkling on the beach, and still they had seen no signs of a dance.

"I can't understand it," said the Lobster. "Alice said I was to walk until I met her, and she'd take me to the party. And we certainly have been walking a long time."

"We have," agreed Uncle Wiggily. "It is so late I'm afraid I'll have to leave you and go home to supper, as I promised Nurse Jane."

"That's too bad," went on the Lobster. "I wanted you to see how well I can dance on the end of my tail. But I can't understand why we don't get to the quadrille. We certainly have walked down the beach, haven't we?"

"We have," answered the bunny. "But—Ah! I have it!" Uncle Wiggily suddenly cried. "You have been walking BACKWARD, and I have been following you. We have been going away from the dance instead of toward it."

"Of course!" cried the Lobster, in a cold and clammy voice. "Why didn't I think of that before? I always have to go backward, on account of my claws being so heavy I have to pull them after me, instead of pushing them ahead.

"And so, of course, going backward as I do, and as all Lobsters do, when I want to get anywhere I always turn my back toward it, and get to it that way. This time I forgot to do that."

"But what can we do now?" Uncle Wiggily wanted to know. "How can we get to the dance?"

"I'll just turn around and back up to it," spoke the Lobster. "I'm sorry to have mixed things up for you, especially as you were so kind as to get me from under the pile of seaweed."

"Oh, don't worry!" laughed Uncle Wiggily, jolly-like. "I dare say it will be all right. Come on!"

So the lobster turned around and began to back toward where he hoped to find the dance. It grew darker and darker, and the star fish were twinkling more than ever, and then, all of a sudden, they came to the hollow stump bungalow where Uncle Wiggily lived.

"Hurray!" cried the Lobster. "Here we are at the quadrille. Now I'll explain to Alice—"

"No, this isn't the dance," said Uncle Wiggily. "This is where I live. But I'd be pleased to have you come in to supper, and we can go to the dance tomorrow."

"I will!" cried the Lobster, after thinking about it.

Into the hollow stump bungalow they went, the Lobster backing in, of course, and Uncle Wiggily cried:

"Supper for two, if you please, Nurse Jane!"

"Right away!" answered the muskrat lady. And she began to set the table. And then, while Uncle Wiggily and the Lobster were talking together Nurse Jane called:

"Oh, dear! I've lost the can opener, and I can't open this tin of peaches. What shall I do?"

"Let me try!" begged Uncle Wiggily. But his paws were not big enough.

"I'll do it!" said the Lobster. And with his strong, pinching claws he punched open the can of peaches as easily as you can eat a chocolate cream drop. It was no trouble at all for him. So it was a good thing Uncle Wiggily brought the Lobster home for supper, you see.

And if the stairs don't stand on their heads and with their toes tickle all the holes out of the lawn tennis nets, I'll tell you next about Uncle Wiggily and Father William.

CHAPTER XIII

UNCLE WIGGILY AND FATHER WILLIAM

One morning, soon after he had finished his breakfast, having taken his red, white and blue striped barber pole rheumatism crutch down from behind the clock, Uncle Wiggily Longears, the rabbit gentleman, started out from his hollow stump bungalow.

There were quite a few friends of the little girl named Alice in Wonderland whom he had not yet met, and he hoped to have an adventure with one of them. So, tossing up in the air his tall silk stovepipe hat, and letting it bounce three times on the end of his pink nose, Uncle Wiggily hurried off.

The rabbit gentleman had not gone very far, over the fields and through the woods, before he saw something very strange indeed. This something was what seemed to be a funny sort of flower vase, with two things sticking up in it, and on the end of them were two shoes.

"My goodness me, sakes alive and some chocolate cake pudding!" cried the surprised bunny uncle. "What's this?"

Then, as he looked again, he saw a funny face, and a pair of bright eyes looking at him from the bottom part of what seemed to be a flower vase.

"Why, it's a man!" cried Uncle Wiggily.

"Of course I'm a man," was the jolly answer. "But don't be afraid of me; I'm not a hunter man."

"And you—you're standing on your head!" went on Uncle Wiggily, more surprised than ever.

"Of course I'm standing on my head!" said the funny man. "I have to do that to make things come out as they do in the Alice in Wonderland book. I'm Father William, you know," and with that he gave a nimble spring, turned a back somersault, putting himself right side up, and began to recite this verse:

"You are old, Father William, the Young Man said,

And your hair has become very white.

But yet you incessantly stand on your head.

Do you think, at your age, that is right?"

"But is it?" asked Uncle Wiggily quickly, as soon as funny Father William had ceased speaking.

"Of course it is," was the answer. "Otherwise it wouldn't be in the book and I wouldn't do it. At first it came very hard to me, but now I can easily manage. And you'll find you get quite a different view of things, looking at them upside down as I do every now and then," he went on.

"I wonder if I could stand on my head?" spoke Uncle Wiggily.

"Try it," said Father William.

"I'd like to," went on the bunny uncle. "But I might crush my tall silk hat."

"Take it off," suggested Father William.

"Yes, I could do that. But suppose some one were to see me?" asked the bunny. "It would look sort of queer."

"No one will see you here behind the trees," spoke Father William. "Besides, if they do, learning to stand on one's head is very useful. There is no telling when you may want to do it at home."

"That's so," agreed Uncle Wiggily. "Well, I'll try."

At first he couldn't stand up on his head at all, just turning over in a sort of flip-flop every time he tried. But at last Father William held up the bunny rabbit by the heels, and then Uncle Wiggily did it better. After a while he could stand straight, right side up, on his hind paws, give a little wiggle, and then suddenly, with a funny twist and a somersault flop, there he was, standing on his head, with his silk hat twirling around on his upper paws. And Father William could do the same thing.

If you had happened to walk through the woods when Uncle Wiggily and Father William, who had a little holiday from the Alice book, were standing on their heads, surely you would have laughed.

"And, now that I have learned a new trick, I must go look for an adventure," said the bunny.

"I'll go with you," spoke Father William. Together they went along through the woods and over the fields and, all of a sudden, from behind a currant jam bush, out jumped a bad, old, double-jointed skillery-scalery alligator.

"Ah, ha!" cried the alligator. "At last I have caught some one to whom I can do it! Ah, ha!"

"Do what?" asked Uncle Wiggily, while Father William looked around for a place to hide. "What are you going to do?"

"Tickle your feet!" was the surprising answer. "I am the ticklish alligator, and feet I must tickle! Get ready now, here I come."

"Oh, dear!" cried Father William. "I never can bear to have my feet tickled. For, when that happens I laugh and then I sneeze and then I catch cold and have to go to bed. Oh, dear! I don't want my feet tickled!"

"Hush!" whispered Uncle Wiggily, as the 'gator was hopping toward them. "You won't have to suffer that! Quick! Stand on your head as you taught me to, and hold your feet up in the air!"

And in the twinkle of a spiced pear Uncle Wiggily and Father William were standing on their heads. The surprised alligator saw them, and after trying to reach their feet with his claws, which he couldn't do, as they were up in the air, he cried:

"Ah, ha! Thought you'd fool me, didn't you, by standing on your heads! Well, I'll tickle your feet after all. I'll climb a tree and reach down to them!"

"Oh, dear! He'll make me catch cold no matter what I do," sighed Father William.

"No, he won't," said Uncle Wiggily. "The alligator is very good at climbing up trees, but it takes him ever so long to climb down. As soon as he climbs up we'll stop standing on our heads. We'll flip-flop to our feet and run away."

And that's exactly what the bunny and Father William did. As soon as the alligator was up in the tree branches they turned a flip-flop, stood up straight and away they ran, and the alligator was all day getting down out of the tree. So he didn't tickle their feet after all, but he might have if Uncle Wiggily had not learned to stand on his head.

And if the ice wagon doesn't slide down hill and throw snowballs at the potato pudding in the parlor I'll tell you next about Uncle Wiggily and the magic bottles.

CHAPTER XIV

UNCLE WIGGILY AND THE MAGIC BOTTLES

Uncle Wiggily Longears, the rabbit gentleman, was hopping along through the woods one morning after having eaten breakfast in his hollow stump bungalow, when, just as he reached a nice, grassy place, near a spring of water, he saw the little flaxen-haired girl, Alice from Wonderland, coming toward him.

"Oh, I'm so glad to see you!" cried Alice. "You are just in time to win the first prize."

She handed the gentleman rabbit a little bottle, filled with what seemed to be water, and stoppered with a blue cork.

"First prize for what?" asked Uncle Wiggily.

"For getting here early," answered Alice. "And you also get second prize, too," and she handed him another bottle, stoppered with a red cork.

"Why do I get second prize?" asked the bunny.

"For not being late," answered Alice with a smile. "It is very simple. First prize for being early, second prize for not being late."

"Hum!" said Uncle Wiggily, sort of scratching his pink, twinkling nose, thoughtful like. "It's much the same thing, it seems to me."

"Not at all," said Alice, quickly. "The prizes are very different. Those bottles are magical. They are filled with water from the pool of tears. If you drink a few drops from the one with the blue cork you will grow very small. And if you take some of the water from the red-stoppered bottle you will grow very large. Be careful of your prizes."

"I will," promised Uncle Wiggily. "Are there any others coming?" he asked, looking about through the trees.

"Any others coming where?" inquired Alice.

"Here. I mean, might they have gotten prizes, too?"

"No, only you," said the flaxen-haired girl. "You were the only one expected."

"But," spoke the puzzled bunny rabbit, "if I was the only one expected, what was the use of giving prizes? No one else could have gotten here ahead of me; could they?"

"Please don't ask me," begged Alice. "All I know is that it's one of the riddles like those the March Hare asks, such as 'What makes the mirror look crooked at you?' The answer is it doesn't if you don't. In this case you get the prizes because there is no one else to give them to. So take them and have an adventure. I have to go see what the Duchess wants."

With that Alice faded away like the Cheshire Cat, beginning at her head and ending up at her feet, the last things to go being the buttons on her shoes.

"Well," said Uncle Wiggily to himself, "I have two prizes, it seems, of magic bottles. I wonder what I am to do with them?"

He looked at the red and blue corked bottles, holding one in each paw, and he was wondering whether it would be best to grow small or large, when, all at once, he felt himself caught from behind by a pair of big claws, and, looking over his shoulder, as best he could, Uncle Wiggily saw that he was held fast by a big alligator; a skillery-scalery chap with a double-jointed tail that he could swing back and forth like a pantry door.

"Ah, ha! I have you!" gurgled the 'gator.

"Yes, I see you have!" said Uncle Wiggily, sadly.

"You thought you and Father William would fool me by standing on your heads so I couldn't tickle your feet," went on the 'gator, as I call him for short. "But I got down out of the tree, and here I am. I have you now and you can't get away from me!"

Indeed it did seem so, for he held Uncle Wiggily very tight and fast in his claws.

"What are you going to do with me?" asked the rabbit.

"Take you home to my den, and my dear little foxes, Eight, Nine and Ten," said the alligator.

"Foxes!" cried Uncle Wiggily. "Have you foxes?"

"I have!" answered the alligator. "I am keeping them until their father gets back from a hunting trip, and they are very hungry. Their father is the fox who went out 'in a hungry plight, and he begged of the moon to give him light, for he'd many miles to go that night, before he could reach his den-O.'"

"Oh, now I remember," said Uncle Wiggily. "It's in Mother Goose."

"Yes, and so is the rest of it," went on the alligator. "'At last the fox reached home to his den, and his dear little foxes, Eight, Nine, Ten.' Those are their names, though they sound like numbers," said the 'gator. "I'll soon introduce you to them. Come along!"

Now Uncle Wiggily did not like this at all. He wanted to get away from the alligator, but he did not know how he could do it. At last he thought of the magical bottles Alice had given him.

"Ah, ha!" thought Uncle Wiggily. "I'll give the alligator a drink from the blue-corked one, and we'll see what happens." So Uncle Wiggily slyly said to the 'gator:

"Before you take me off to your den, would you not like a drink from this bottle to refresh you?"

"Yes, I would," said the skillery-scalery creature, not at all politely. "I was going to take some anyhow whether you asked me or not."

With that he took the blue-corked bottle from the paw of the bunny rabbit gentleman, pulled out the stopper with his teeth and drank a few drops.

And, no sooner had he done that, than the alligator began to shrink. First he became as small as a dog, then as little as a cat, then as tiny as a kitten, then no larger than a bird and finally he was no bigger than a baby angle worm. And when the alligator became that size Uncle Wiggily was not afraid and easily got away from him, taking the two magic bottles.

"Oh, dear!" cried the 'gator in a baby angle worm voice, which was about as loud as the head of a pin. "How foolish I was to drink from the magic bottle and grow small."

But it served him right, I think, and the bunny uncle was safe. And if the head of the table doesn't step on the front door mat and make it slide off the porch I'll tell you next about Uncle Wiggily and the croquet ball.

CHAPTER XV

UNCLE WIGGILY AND THE CROQUET BALL

"Why in the world are you taking those bottles with you?" asked Nurse Jane Fuzzy Wuzzy, the muskrat lady housekeeper, as she saw Uncle Wiggily, the bunny rabbit gentleman, hopping off the front porch of his hollow stump bungalow one morning.

"These are the prizes which Alice from Wonderland gave me," answered Mr. Longears, as he looked at the blue and red corked bottles. "The red one makes things grow larger and the blue one makes them smaller. I am going to take them with me as I go looking for an adventure today, as there is no telling when I might need them. I did yesterday, when the alligator caught me. I gave him a drink from the blue bottle and he shrunk until he was no larger than a baby angle worm."

The rabbit gentleman had not gone very far, twinkling his pink nose as he hopped, before, all of a sudden, he came to a place where a big stone grew out of the ground, and near it he heard a voice, saying:

"Oh, dear! Oh, dear! Oh, dear!"

"Ha! That sounds like trouble!" exclaimed the bunny. "Who are you and what is the matter?" he asked, kindly.

"Oh, I am a Lady Bug," was the answer, "and I am so small that I either get lost all the while, or all the other animals and bugs in the forest step on me. Oh, I wish I were larger so I could be more easily seen!"

"Indeed, you are rather hard to see," said Uncle Wiggily, and he had to look twice through his glasses before he could notice the Lady Bug. At the first look he only half saw her, but the second time he saw her fully.

"I'd like to be about as large as a June Beetle," said the Lady Bug. "But I don't s'pose I ever shall be."

"Oh, yes you will!" cried jolly Uncle Wiggily.

"I will! How?" asked the Lady Bug, eagerly.

"I have here some water in a magic bottle," said the bunny. "I'll give you a few drops of it, and it will make you grow larger." So he took some water from the red-corked flask, and let the Lady Bug sip it. Instantly she grew as large as a turkey.

"Oh, now I'm too big," she said.

"I see you are," said Uncle Wiggily.

"I'll have to give you some from the other bottle and make you grow smaller." So he did, but he must have given a little too much, for the Lady Bug suddenly grew as small as the point of a baby pin.

"Oh, this is worse and worse," she said sadly.

"I know it!" agreed Uncle Wiggily. "Wait, I'll give you a little of both kinds," and he did, so the Lady Bug grew to the size of a small potato, which was just right, so she would not get lost or stepped on.

After the Lady Bug had thanked him, Uncle Wiggily, with his two magical bottles, hopped on through the woods. He had not gone very far before he saw Alice of Wonderland and the Queen of Hearts playing croquet on a grassy place.

"Come on, Uncle Wiggily!" called Alice. "You're just in time for the game."

"Fine!" said the bunny uncle, taking a mallet and round wooden ball which the Queen handed him.

"Three strikes and you go out!" warned the Queen.

"What does she mean?" asked Uncle Wiggily of Alice. "This isn't baseball."

"She means," explained the little flaxen-haired girl, "that if you miss striking the croquet ball three times with your mallet you have to go out and bring in some ice cream."

"Oh, I shan't mind that," the bunny rabbit said. "In fact, I shall rather like it. Now, what do I do — ?"

"Play ball!" suddenly cried the Queen of Hearts, and she struck with her mallet the croquet ball near her such a hard blow that it sailed through the air and hit Uncle Wiggily in the coat tails. And then something cracked.

All at once the croquet ball began growing larger! Bigger and bigger it grew, like a snowball which you roll in the yard, and then it began to roll after Uncle Wiggily. Down the croquet ground the big wooden ball chased after him, rolling closer and closer.

"Oh, my!" cried the Queen of Hearts, "What have I done?"

"The ball cracked the magical red stoppered bottle that was in my coat tail pocket!" cried Uncle Wiggily over his shoulder, as he ran. "Some of the magic, big-growing water spilled on the ball, and now it has turned into a giant! Oh, it will crush me!"

And, really, it did seem as though the big croquet ball would, for now it was as large as a house and still growing, so strong was the water in the magical bottle that had been broken.

Larger and larger grew the croquet ball, and faster and faster it rolled after Uncle Wiggily. It was almost on his heels now, and the bunny gentleman was running so fast that his tall silk hat flew off.

"Oh, what shall I do?" he cried.

Alice thought for a minute, then she called:

"Quick, Uncle Wiggily. Take out the blue-corked bottle and sprinkle some of that water on the croquet ball! Hurry now!"

Uncle Wiggily did. As he ran he turned and threw back over his shoulder some of the blue bottle water on the big rolling croquet ball. And, all at once, just as the alligator had done, the croquet ball shrank and shrank until it was no larger than a boy's marble, and then it couldn't hurt Uncle Wiggily even if it did roll on him.

But it is a good thing he had that bottle of shrinking water with him; isn't it?

And, if the expressman doesn't take the baby carriage to ride the trunk down to the five-and-ten-cent store to buy a new piano, I'll tell you next about Uncle Wiggily and the Do-do.

CHAPTER XVI
UNCLE WIGGILY AND THE DO-DO

"I declare!" exclaimed Nurse Jane Fuzzy Wuzzy, the muskrat lady housekeeper for Uncle Wiggily Longears, the rabbit gentleman, "I declare, I'll never get it done — never!"

"What?" asked Uncle Wiggily. "What won't you get done?"

"All this housework," answered Miss Fuzzy Wuzzy. "You see, going over to call on Mrs. Bushytail, the squirrel lady, last night I didn't wash the supper dishes, and now I have them to do, and also the breakfast dishes and the sweeping and dusting and I ought to bake a cake, and mend some of your socks and —"

"Whoa!" called Uncle Wiggily with a jolly laugh, as though he had spoken to Munchie Trot, the pony. "That's enough! Don't say any more. You have too much work to do."

"And I'm worried about it," said Nurse Jane.

"Don't be," advised the rabbit gentleman. "I'll stay and help you do it."

"No," said Nurse Jane. "Thank you just the same, but I'd rather you wouldn't stay around the hollow stump bungalow when there is so much to do. You might get in my way and I'd step on you. That would give me the fidgets. It is very kind of you, but if you'll go off and have an adventure I think that will be best."

"Just as you say," agreed Uncle Wiggily. "But I'd like to help. Can't I bring you a diamond dishpan or a gold wash rag from the five and ten cent store?"

"No! Hop along with you!" laughed Nurse Jane. "I dare say I'll manage somehow."

So Uncle Wiggily hopped along, over the fields and through the woods, and then he suddenly said to himself:

"I know what I'll do. I'll play a little trick on Nurse Jane. She shouldn't spend so much time in the kitchen. A little is all right, but there is too much trouble about housework. Here I go off and have an adventure and she has to slop around in dishwater. It isn't right!"

Then the rabbit gentleman hopped along until he came to a woodland telephone, made from a trumpet vine flower, and into that he called, speaking right into his own hollow stump bungalow and to Nurse Jane.

"Oh, Miss Fuzzy Wuzzy!" called Uncle Wiggily. "Can you come over to Mrs. Wibblewobble's duck house right away?"

"Why, yes, I can," answered the muskrat lady, "though I have a lot of work to do. What is the matter?"

"I'll tell you when you get there," said the voice of Uncle Wiggily, pretending he was Mrs. Wibblewobble, the duck lady. Then he called up Mrs. Wibblewobble herself, told her how he had fooled Nurse Jane, and asked the duck lady, when the muskrat lady housekeeper came, to keep her talking and visiting as long as she could.

"And while Nurse Jane is at your house, Mrs. Wibblewobble," said Uncle Wiggily, over the trumpet vine telephone, "I'll run around the back way to the hollow stump bungalow and do all the work."

"That will be a nice surprise for Nurse Jane," the duck lady said.

Uncle Wiggily guessed so, too, and when he thought Nurse Jane was safely at Mrs. Wibblewobble's house, he went to the bungalow. He took off his tall silk hat, laid aside his red, white and blue striped rheumatism crutch, and began with the dishes. There was a large pile of them, but Uncle Wiggily was brave.

"When I was a soldier I fought a great many more mosquitoes than there are dishes here," he said. "I will make believe the plates, cups and saucers are the enemy, and I will charge on them and souse them."

And Uncle Wiggily did, with a cake of soap for a gun and washing powder to fire with. But, still and with all, there were many dishes, and when he thought of the beds to make, the sweeping and dusting to be done and the socks to mend, Uncle Wiggily said:

"Oh, dear!"

"What's the matter?" asked a voice behind him, and turning, he saw Alice from Wonderland. With her was a queer bird, which had a tail like that of a mouse.

"Oh, I'm glad to see you!" said Uncle Wiggily. "But I can't go and have an adventure with you, Alice, as I have to do all these dishes. Then I have to do the sweeping and do the dusting and do—"

"That's enough!" laughed Alice. "There are too many Do-dos. I am just in time, I see. My friend will help you," and she pointed to the queer bird.

"What?" cried Uncle Wiggily. "Can he do dishes?"

"He can do anything!" laughed Alice. "He is the Do-do bird, and all I have to do is to pinch his tail and he will work very fast."

"Doesn't it hurt him?" asked Uncle Wiggily.

"What, to work fast?" Alice wanted to know.

"No, to pinch his tail."

"Not in the least," answered Alice. "He's used to it. The only trouble is I have to keep on pinching it to make him do things, and that means I have to keep my finger and thumb on his tail all the while and follow him around. Now we'll begin to do things, dear Do-do," and she pinched the bird's tail.

At once the bird began to wash dishes, and soon they were all done, and then when the Do-do started to do the beds Uncle Wiggily thought of a new plan.

"As long as you have to pinch his tail," said the bunny to Alice, "I'll get Nurse Jane's hair curlers. You can snap them on his tail and they'll keep pinching on it, and pinching on it all the while, and you and I can go take a walk."

"Fine!" cried Alice. So with the hair curlers pinching his tail the Do-do bird quickly did all the bungalow housework, and Uncle Wiggily and Alice had a fine walk. And when Nurse Jane came home from Mrs. Wibblewobble's and found the work all done she was very happy. And so was the Do-do, for he loved to do dishes.

And if the teacup doesn't try to hide in the milk pitcher, where the bread crumbs can't tickle it when they play tag with the butter knife, I'll tell you next about Uncle Wiggily and the Lory.

CHAPTER XVII

UNCLE WIGGILY AND THE LORY

Once upon a time the skillery-scalery alligator was out walking in the fields near the muddy river where he lived, and he happened to meet a big spider.

"Good morning, Mr. Alligator," said Mr. Spider. "Have you caught that Uncle Wiggily Longears bunny yet?"

"I have not, I am sorry to say," answered the alligator chap. "I've tried every way I know how, but something always happens so that he gets away. Either he is helped by that funny book-girl, Alice from Wonderland, or by some of her friends. I'm afraid I'll never catch Uncle Wiggily."

"Oh, yes, you will," said Mr. Spider. "I'll help you."

"How?" asked the 'gator, which was his short name, though he was rather long.

"I'll crawl through the woods and over the fields until I find him asleep," said Mr. Spider. "And, when I do, I'll spin a strong web around and over him so he cannot get loose. Then I'll come and tell you and you can get him."

"Very good," spoke Mr. Alligator. "Please do it."

So the alligator went back to sleep in the mud to wait until Mr. Spider should bring him word that Uncle Wiggily was held fast in the web.

And now let us see what happens to the bunny gentleman. As he always did, he started out from his hollow stump bungalow one morning to look for an adventure. There had been a little accident at breakfast time. Nurse Jane Fuzzy Wuzzy, the muskrat lady housekeeper, had boiled the eggs too long and they were as hard as bullets.

"You can't eat them," she said to Uncle Wiggily. "I'll boil you some fresh ones."

"All right," laughed the bunny. "I don't want to get indyspepsia by eating hard bullet eggs. But I'll take them with me and give them to Johnnie or

Billie Bushytail, the squirrel boys. They can crack hard nuts so they must be able to crack hard boiled eggs."

So it was that Uncle Wiggily, after having eaten the newly boiled soft eggs, started from his hollow stump bungalow with the hard boiled eggs in his pocket.

He had not traveled very far before he heard from behind a big log a voice crying:

"Oh, dear! It isn't hard enough! It isn't half hard enough!"

"What isn't?" asked Uncle Wiggily, as he saw a funny looking bird with a very large bill like a parrot's. "What isn't hard enough?"

"This log of wood," was the answer. "I need something hard to bite on to sharpen my beak, but this wood is too soft."

"You are a funny bird," laughed the bunny gentleman. "Who might you be?"

"I am the Lory bird," was the answer. "I belong in the book with Alice of Wonderland, but I'm out for a day's pleasure, and, as I can't tell what I might have to eat, I thought I'd sharpen my bill. But I can't find anything hard enough to use as a grindstone."

"Suppose you try these," said Uncle Wiggily, taking the hard boiled eggs out of his pocket.

"The very thing!" cried the Lory. "These will be fine for my bill!" With that he champed his beak down on the hard eggs and he had all he could do to bite them. "Now I'll get my beak good and sharp," said Lory. "You have done me a great favor, Uncle Wiggily, and I hope some day to do you one."

"Pray, do not mention it," said the bunny rabbit, modest-like and shy. Then, having found a good use for the hard boiled eggs, even if he didn't give them to the Bushytail squirrel boys, Uncle Wiggily hopped along, and the Lory kept on biting the shells for practice.

Now, it was a warm day, and, as Uncle Wiggily felt tired, he sat down in a shady place in the fields, and soon fell fast asleep. And, no sooner was he in Dreamland than along came Mr. Spider.

"Ah, ha!" said the spider. "Now's my chance to catch this bunny for the alligator. I'll spin a strong web around him, so strong that he cannot break loose. Then I'll go get my friend, the 'gator."

So while Uncle Wiggily slept, Mr. Spider spun a strong web about the bunny — a very extra strong web, with such big strands that Uncle Wiggily never could have broken them himself. And when the web was all finished, and the bunny was helpless, he awakened just as Mr. Spider was going off to call Mr. Alligator.

"Oh, what has happened to me?" cried the bunny, as he found he could not move his paws or even twinkle his pink nose. "Oh, what is it? Let me go!"

"No, you can't go!" said the spider. "You are going to stay there until I bring Mr. Alligator," and away he crawled. Uncle Wiggily tried to get loose, but he could not.

"Oh, if only some one would come who's good and strong, and would cut this web, then I would be free!" said the bunny.

And then, all of a sudden, out from behind the bush came the Four and Twenty Tailors, from Mother Goose. They had their big scissors with them, and they were led by Alice of Wonderland.

"I told these silly tailors I'd help them hunt the snail, because they are so timid that they even fear her tail," laughed Alice, "but we'll stop and help you first, dear Uncle Wiggily!"

Then the Four and Twenty Tailors, with their shears, sniped and snapped the strong spider's web until it was all in pieces and the bunny could easily get loose. And when the alligator, fetched by the spider, came to get the bunny he wasn't there.

But the strong-billed Lory bird was there. He had heard about Uncle Wiggily's trouble from the Do-do bird, and had come, with his strong bill, to bite the spider web into little pieces.

"But I am too late, I see," said the Lory. "The Mother Goose Tailors got here first. However, as I want to bite something hard and mean I'll bite the alligator." And he did and the alligator said "Ouch!" and I'm glad of it.

And if the telephone bell doesn't ring at the front door and make believe it's the milkman looking for old rags, I'll tell you next about Uncle Wiggily and the puppy.

CHAPTER XVIII

UNCLE WIGGILY AND THE PUPPY

"Oh, Uncle Wiggily! Oh, Uncle Wiggily! Oh, Uncle Wiggily!" called Jackie and Peetie Bow Wow, the two doggie boys, as they ran barking up to the hollow stump bungalow one morning.

"Well, well! What's the matter now?" asked Uncle Wiggily Longears, the rabbit gentleman, as he came out on the porch.

"Oh, we've got a baby over at our house!" cried Jackie.

"Come and see it!" barked Peetie.

"A baby? At your house?" exclaimed Uncle Wiggily.

"Well, a little puppy dog," said Jackie. "That's the same to us as a real baby is to real persons."

"To be sure," agreed the bunny uncle. "I'll come over and see the new baby puppy," and putting on his tall silk hat, and taking down his red-white-and-blue-striped barber pole rheumatism crutch from the electric light, Mr. Longears started away over the fields to the kennel house, where the Bow Wow dog family lived.

"There's the new baby puppy!" cried Jackie, as he poked away the straw from the bed where something was moving about.

"I—why, bless my spectacles—I can hardly see him!" said Uncle Wiggily, taking off his glasses to polish them, for he thought maybe he had splashed some carrot oatmeal on them at breakfast and that they were clouded over.

"He's so small, that's why you can't see him," spoke Peetie. "But he'll soon grow big like us, Uncle Wiggily."

"Let us hope so," spoke the bunny uncle. "He's so small now I'd be afraid of stepping on him if I lived here."

"He's got awful cute eyes," said Peetie. "They aren't open yet, but I can pull 'em apart a little bit to show you they're going to be blue color, I guess," and Peetie began opening the shut eyes of his little baby brother puppy. Of course, the puppy whined and Mrs. Bow Wow called:

"Now, what are you boys doing to that baby?"

"Nothing, ma," answered Jackie.

"We're jest pokin' open his eyes so Uncle Wiggily can see 'em," answered Peetie.

"Oh, you doggie boys!" cried Mrs. Bow Wow. "You mustn't do that! I'm glad Uncle Wiggily came to see our baby, but now you run out and play, Peetie and Jackie, while I visit with Mr. Longears."

So the doggie boys ran out to play with Johnnie and Billie Bushytail, the squirrels, and Mrs. Bow Wow told Uncle Wiggily what a nice baby Wuff-Wuff was. Wuff-Wuff was the new puppy's name.

"I'm sure he'll grow up to be a fine dog," said the bunny. Just then the telephone bell in the kennel house rang, and when Mrs. Bow Wow answered she said, after listening awhile:

"Oh, dear! This is your friend Nurse Jane Fuzzy Wuzzy talking to me. She wants me to come over to show her how to make a strawberry longcake, as there is a lot of company coming for supper. A short cake won't be large enough."

"Are you going to my hollow stump bungalow?" asked Uncle Wiggily.

"I'd like to, only I can't leave Baby Wuff Wuff," said Mrs. Bow Wow.

"Oh, I'll stay and take care of him," said the bunny uncle. "I think I can do it, and it may be an adventure for me. Trot along, Mrs. Bow Wow."

"Very well, I will. If Wuff Wuff gets hungry, just give him some milk from this bottle," and she handed a nursing one to Uncle Wiggily. So Mrs. Bow Wow went over to help Nurse Jane, the muskrat lady housekeeper, make the longcake, and the bunny man stayed with the puppy baby.

Uncle Wiggily sat in the kennel house, while the little doggie nestled in the straw. The bunny rabbit was just wondering who the company could be that were coming to his bungalow, when, all of a sudden, there was a big noise outside the kennel, and a big voice cried:

"Now I know you're in there, Uncle Wiggily, for I saw you hop in with Jackie and Peetie. And I know they're gone, for I saw them go out. And I know Mrs. Bow Wow is out. So you're there all alone and I'm going to get you!" And Uncle Wiggily saw the big skillery-scalery alligator standing outside the door.

"Oh, my!" thought the bunny rabbit gentleman. "He'll surely get me this time, for he can knock the kennel house apart with one flip-flap of his double-jointed tail. But maybe, if I keep real still, he will think I'm gone."

So Uncle Wiggily snuggled down in the straw with the baby puppy, but the alligator cried:

"Oh, I know you're there, and I'm going to get you!"

"Oh, if only this puppy was a big, strong dog, like Nero!" thought Uncle Wiggily, "he could save me from the alligator." Just then the puppy began to whine, and the bunny rabbit said:

"Oh, don't do that, Wuff Wuff! Don't whine, and make a noise, or the alligator will get you, too."

But the puppy baby still whined, for he was hungry. Uncle Wiggily picked up a bottle and put the end of it in Wuff Wuff's mouth.

"Here, drink that," said the bunny. "Then you won't be hungry." The puppy baby did so, and then something very strange happened. The little puppy suddenly began growing very large. First he was the size of Mr. Bow Wow, and then he swelled up until he was as big as a horse, and had to get out of the kennel house for fear of bursting off the roof.

And when the alligator saw the great big puppy dog, like the one in Alice of Wonderland, suddenly standing in front of him, Mr. 'Gator just gave one flip of his tail, and away he ran crying:

"Oh, my! I didn't know an elephant was there to save Uncle Wiggily!"

But there wasn't. It was only the puppy who had suddenly grown big. For by mistake instead of giving him the bottle of milk, the bunny rabbit gave him some of the water from the magical red-stoppered, big-growing bottle that Alice from Wonderland had sent the bunny. It had been mended after the croquet ball broke it. And, after the puppy had scared away the alligator, Uncle Wiggily gave Wuff Wuff some water from the magical blue-stoppered bottle and shrunk him to his regular baby size, and everybody was happy.

And if the fairy tale doesn't waggle itself all around the book case and scare all the big words out of the dictionary, I'll tell you next about Uncle Wiggily and the Unicorn.

CHAPTER XIX

UNCLE WIGGILY AND THE UNICORN

"Well, you look just as if you were going somewhere, Uncle Wiggily," said Nurse Jane Fuzzy Wuzzy, the muskrat lady housekeeper, as the rabbit gentleman whizzed around the corner of his hollow stump bungalow in his automobile, with the bologna sausage tires, one morning.

"I am going somewhere," he answered, and really he was, for the wheels were whizzing around like anything.

"And going where, may I ask?" politely inquired the muskrat lady.

"I am going to give Alice a ride," answered Uncle Wiggily. "Alice from Wonderland, I mean. She never has ridden in an automobile."

"She never has?" cried Nurse Jane, in surprise.

"Never! You see, when she was put in that nice book, which tells so much about her, there weren't any autos, and, of course, she never could have had a ride in one.

"But she had ever so many other nice adventures, such as going down the rabbit hole and through the looking glass. However, I promised her a ride in my auto, and here I go to give it to her," and with that Uncle Wiggily sprinkled some pepper and salt on the sausage tires of his auto's wheels to make them go faster.

The rabbit gentleman found Alice, the little book girl, in the White Queen's garden having a make-believe tea party with the Mock Turtle, who soon would have to go into the 5 o'clock soup.

"Oh, how kind of you to come for me, Uncle Wiggily!" cried Alice, and she jumped up so quickly that she overturned the multiplication table, at which she and the Mock Turtle had been sitting, and ran to jump in the auto.

"Well, I don't call that very nice," said the Mock Turtle. "Here she's gone and mixed up the seven times table with the three times six, and goodness knows when I'll ever get them straightened out again."

"I'm sorry!" called Alice, waving her hand as she rode off with Uncle Wiggily. "I'll help you when I come back."

"And I'll help too," promised the bunny uncle.

Mr. Longears and Wonderland Alice rode over the fields and through the woods, and they were having a fine time when, all of a sudden, as the automobile came near a place where some oak trees grew in a thick cluster Alice cried:

"Hark! They're fighting!"

"Who?" asked Uncle Wiggily. "Please don't tell me it is the mosquito enemy coming after me to bite me."

"No, it's the Lion and the Unicorn," Alice answered. "Don't you remember how it goes in my book:

"'The Lion and the Unicorn were fighting for the Crown,

The Lion beat the Unicorn all around the town.

Some gave them white bread, some gave them brown,

And then the funny Unicorn jumped right up and down.'

"That last line isn't just right," explained Alice to the bunny uncle, "but I couldn't properly think of it, I'm so frightened!"

"Frightened? At what" asked Uncle Wiggily.

"At the Unicorn," answered Alice. "Here he comes," and, as she said that, Uncle Wiggily saw a funny animal, like a horse, with a big long horn sticking out of the middle of his head, straight in front of him, galloping out of the clump of trees.

"Hurray! I beat him!" cried the Unicorn. "Come on now, quick, I must get away from here before they catch me!"

"You beat him? Do you mean beat the Lion?" asked Uncle Wiggily for he was not frightened as was Alice.

"Sure I beat him," answered the Unicorn, as he jumped into the back seat of the automobile. "Drive on!" he ordered just as if the bunny uncle gentleman were the coachman.

"Did you beat him very hard, with a broomstick?" asked Alice, putting out her head from behind Uncle Wiggily's tall silk hat where she had hidden herself.

"Beat him with a broomstick? Ha! Ha! I should say not!" laughed the Unicorn. "We're too jolly good friends for that," and he spoke like an English chap. "I beat him playing hop-Scotch and Jack-straws. I was two hops and three straws ahead of him when I stopped and ran away because they were after me."

"Who were after you?" asked Alice. "The lion's friends?"

"No, the straws that show which way the wind blows. When the wind blows the straws against me they tickle, and I can't bear to be tickled. I'm worse than a soap bubble that way. So I ran to get in the auto. I hope you don't mind," and the Unicorn leaned back on the seat cushions.

"Mind? Not in the least!" cried Uncle Wiggily. "I'm glad to give you a ride with Alice," and he made the auto go very fast. On and on they went, over the fields and through the woods and then, all of a sudden, out from behind a tree jumped the big skillery-scalery alligator walking on his hind legs and the end of his double-jointed tail.

"Halt!" he cried, like a sentry soldier, and Uncle Wiggily stopped the auto. "At last I have caught you," said the alligator in a nutmeg grater sort of a voice. "I want you, Uncle Wiggily, and that Alice girl also. As for your friend in the back seat, he may go — "

"Oh, may I? Thank you!" cried the Unicorn, and with that he leaned forward. And, as he did so the long sharp horn in his head reached over Uncle Wiggily's shoulder, and began to tickle the alligator right under his soft ribs.

"Oh, stop! Stop it, I tell you!" giggled the 'gator. "Stop tickling me!" and he laughed and wiggled and squirmed like an angle worm going fishing.

"Stop! Stop!" he begged.

"I will when you let my friends, Uncle Wiggily and Alice, alone," said the Unicorn, still tickling away.

"Yes! Yes! I'll let them alone," promised the alligator, and he laughed until the tears ran down his tail. And then he had to run off by himself through the woods, and so he didn't get the bunny uncle nor Wonderland Alice either. And he never could have gotten the Unicorn, because of his long, ticklish horn.

So it is sometimes a good thing to take one of these stickery chaps along when you go for an automobile ride. And if the skyrocket doesn't fall down and stub its nose when it tries to jump over the moon with the crumpled horn cow, I'll tell you next about Uncle Wiggily and Humpty Dumpty.

CHAPTER XX
UNCLE WIGGILY AND HUMPTY DUMPTY

"Excuse me," spoke a gentle voice behind Nurse Jane Fuzzy Wuzzy, the muskrat lady housekeeper, who was cleaning the steps of the hollow stump bungalow one morning. "Excuse me, but can Uncle Wiggily be out to play?"

"Be out to play?" repeated Nurse Jane. "Do you mean play with you?" and the muskrat lady turned to see a little girl, with flaxen hair, standing at the foot of the steps.

"Yes, play with me, if you please," said the little girl. "I'm Alice from Wonderland, you know, and Uncle Wiggily and I had such a jolly time yesterday, when the Unicorn tickled the alligator and made him laugh, that I'd like to go off with him again."

"With whom — the alligator?" asked Nurse Jane.

"No, with Uncle Wiggily," laughed Alice. "Where is he?"

"Here I am, Alice. I've just finished breakfast," answered the bunny rabbit gentleman himself, as he came out on the front bungalow steps. "Are you ready for another auto ride?"

"Indeed I am, thank you. And as tomorrow is a holiday I don't have any school today."

"That's funny," said Uncle Wiggily, twinkling his pink nose. "What holiday is it?"

"The Fourth of July!" answered Alice. "Have you forgotten? Even though I am an English girl I know what it means. Your boys and girls shoot off lollypops, bang ice cream cones and light red, white and blue candy."

"Candy? I guess you mean candles!" laughed Uncle Wiggily. "However, you're right. It is the Fourth of July tomorrow, and whereas, years ago, we used to shoot off firecrackers (when many children were burned), now we have a nicer holiday.

"We go off in the woods and gather flowers. Why, do you know!" cried the bunny uncle, "there are flowers just right for Fourth of July. There are puff balls that are as good as torpedoes, and snap-dragons that open their mouths and make believe bite you, and there are dogwood flowers that bark, and red sumach which is just the color of firecrackers."

"Then let's go off in the woods and have Fourth of July there," proposed Alice, and soon she and the bunny uncle were in the automobile. And then along came Sammie and Susie Littletail, the rabbit children, and Johnnie and Billie Bushytail, the squirrels, and Jackie and Peetie Bow Wow, the puppy dogs.

"Oh, Uncle Wiggily!" cried these animal boys and girls. "Take us with you for Fourth of July!"

"Of course I shall!" promised the bunny gentleman, so they all got in the automobile with him and Wonderland Alice, and away they went.

They had not gone very far before, all of a sudden, they came to a stone wall, and when Alice saw something on top of it, she cried:

"Why, there's my old friend Humpty Dumpty. I must stop and speak to him or he'll think I'm proud," and she waved her hands.

"Why, that—that's nothing but an—egg!" said Sammie. "It's like the ones I colored for Easter when the skilli-gimink dye splashed all over me. That isn't Humpty Dumpty at all—it's an egg!"

"Hush!" whispered Susie. "Humpty Dumpty is an egg, of course, but he doesn't like to be told of it. Don't you know the little verse?

"'Humpty Dumpty sat on the wall,

Humpty Dumpty had a great fall.

All the King's horses and all the King's men

Couldn't put Humpty Dumpty together again.'"

"That's right," said Alice from Wonderland. "Only don't speak of the fall before Humpty. He doesn't like to be reminded of it."

"I don't see why," spoke Jackie Bow Wow. "He can't hear a word we say. He's only an egg—he hasn't any ears."

"He really isn't dressed yet," said Alice. "It's a bit early. But I'll soon make him look more human."

With that she jumped out of the auto and, taking two ears of corn from a field nearby, she fastened them with silk from the cob, one on each side of the egg.

"Now he can hear," said Alice. Then with tulip flowers she made Humpty a mouth and from a potato she took two eyes, so the egg could see. A comb made him as nice teeth as one could wish for, and they never ached, and for a nose she took out a cute little bottle of perfumery.

"I think that's a queer nose," said Johnnie Bushytail, frisking his tail.

"Well, a bottle of perfumery smells, doesn't it?" asked Alice, "and that's what a nose is especially for; smells."

"Indeed it is!" cried Humpty Dumpty in his jolly voice, speaking through the tulips. "I'm all made now. I only hope—" And then he suddenly turned pale, for he nearly fell off the wall. "Has any one any powder?" he asked. "I think I'd like to clean my teeth."

"I have some talcum," spoke Lulu Wibblewobble, the duck girl, coming along just then.

"That will do," spoke Humpty Dumpty. "It will be just fine." And with a brush made from the end of a soft fern he began to clean his teeth with the talcum powder which Lulu gave him.

And then, all of a sudden, there was a loud noise, a puff of smoke, and Humpty Dumpty, the egg man, was seen sailing off through the air like a big white balloon.

"Well, this is better than falling off the wall!" he cried in a faint voice.

"Oh, my! What happened?" asked Sammie Littletail, trying to make his pink nose twinkle as Uncle Wiggily did his.

"Humpty Dumpty was blown up instead of falling down," said Alice. "I guess your talcum powder was too strong for him, Lulu, my dear. And it being the Fourth of July tomorrow, Humpty wanted to give us some fireworks. So he's gone, but I'm glad he wasn't broken, for if he was the way the book has it, when he falls off the wall, all the King's horses and all the King's men couldn't put him together again. Maybe it is best as it is."

But, after a while Humpty Dumpty sailed back again, not hurt a bit, and he sat on the wall as well as ever.

Then Alice and Uncle Wiggily and the animal boys and girls had fun in the woods. And, if the pink pills don't hide in the green bottle and pretend they're peppermint candy for the rag doll, I'll tell you next about Uncle Wiggily and the looking glass.

CHAPTER XXI

UNCLE WIGGILY AND THE LOOKING GLASS

"A package came for you while you were out adventuring today," said Nurse Jane Fuzzy Wuzzy, the muskrat lady housekeeper, to Uncle Wiggily Longears, the bunny rabbit gentleman, as he hopped down the stairs of the hollow stump bungalow to breakfast one morning.

"I wonder what's in it?" asked the bunny as he put a slice of carrot jam on his bread and held it over the lettuce coffee to have it flavored.

"I don't know. You'll have to open it to find out," answered Nurse Jane. "It is marked 'Glass. With Care.'"

Uncle Wiggily was so eager and excited like that he could not wait to finish his breakfast, but quickly opened the package which Mr. Hummingbird, the lightning express messenger, had left at the bungalow early that morning.

"It's a looking glass!" exclaimed the bunny uncle when he saw what it was. "And it's from Alice in Wonderland—at least she used to live in Wonderland before she came to Woodland to have adventures with me."

"And there's a note with it," spoke Nurse Jane, as she saw a piece of white birch bark, with writing on it; the letters having been made with a burned stick which marks black like a lead pencil.

"Yes, it's a little letter," said Uncle Wiggily as he read it. "And it's from Alice. It says: 'Dear Uncle Wiggily: I send you the Looking Glass I once went through, and on the other side I had many adventures. I wish you the same!'"

"That's queer," said the bunny, as he turned the glass over and looked at the back. "I don't see any hole where Alice went through."

"Maybe it closed up after her, the same as fairy doors always close once you pass through," explained Nurse Jane.

"I believe you are right," said Uncle Wiggily. "But this is a very small glass for a girl like Alice to get through," and indeed the glass was one of the kind you hold in your hand.

"Maybe the glass was larger when Alice went through it," said Nurse Jane, "or else perhaps she had taken some drops from the magic bottle and grew small like a rubber doll."

"I guess that was it," agreed Uncle Wiggily. "Anyhow, it is very kind of her to send me the looking glass. I may have an adventure with it. I'll take it out on the front steps and then we'll see what happens next."

So, having finished his breakfast, the bunny went out on the bungalow porch and sat with the looking glass in his paw, waiting for something to happen.

He sat there and sat there and sat there and he was just beginning to wonder if anything would happen, when, all of a sudden, there was a rustling in the bushes, and up on the porch popped a bad old skillery-scalery alligator, with bumps all down the middle of his back like the buttons on a lady's dress.

"Ah, ha! I am just in time, I see!" exclaimed the 'gator.

"For what?" asked Uncle Wiggily, suddenly awakening, for he had fallen into a little sleep while he waited for an adventure to happen with the looking glass. "In time for what?"

"To go away with you," answered the alligator.

"But I am not going away," said the bunny. "At least I did not know I was going," and he looked around rather sad and lonesome, for he did not like the bad alligator, and he wanted to see, Uncle Wiggily did, if brave Nurse Jane Fuzzy would not come out and throw cold water on him — on the alligator, I mean — to drive him away. But the muskrat lady had gone to the store to get some cheese for supper.

"I am not going away," said Uncle Wiggily again.

"Oh, yes you are!" exclaimed the alligator, and he smiled in such a way that it seemed as though the whole top of his head would pop off, so large was the smile. "You may not know it, but you are going away, Uncle Wiggily."

"With whom?" asked the bunny.

"With me," answered the 'gator. "We are going away together. I came on purpose to fetch you. Come along," and with that the bad alligator wound his double-jointed tail around the bunny uncle's ears, lifted him out of the rocking chair and started to walk off the bungalow porch with him.

"Oh, stop it!" cried Uncle Wiggily. "Let me go! Let me go!"

"No! No!" barked the alligator, like a dog. "I'll not let you go, now I have you!" and he started to drag the bunny uncle off to the dark, damp, dismal swamp, where the mosquitoes lived with the tent caterpillars.

"Oh, please don't take me away!" begged the bunny. "I wish some one would help me!" and as he said that the alligator gave him a sudden twist and the looking glass, which Uncle Wiggily still held in his paw, came around in front of the alligator's face.

And, no sooner had the 'gator looked in the glass than he gave a loud cry, and, unwinding his tail from Uncle Wiggily, away the bad creature scurried, leaving the bunny alone and safe. And the alligator cried:

"Oh, excuse me! I didn't mean anything! I'll be good! I won't hurt Uncle Wiggily!"

"Well, I wonder what frightened him away?" asked Uncle Wiggily, out loud.

"Seeing himself in the looking glass," was the answer, and there stood Alice from Wonderland. "That is a magical mirror I sent you, Uncle Wiggily," she explained. "It shows the reflection of anything and anybody just as they are and not as they'd like to be.

"And the alligator is such a mean-looking and ugly chap, that, never before having seen himself, this time when he did, in the looking glass, he was frightened, seeing himself as others see him. He thought he was looking at a Chinese dragon who would bite him. So he ran away, leaving you alone."

"And I'm so glad he did," said Uncle Wiggily. "It's a good thing I had your looking glass."

Then Alice and Uncle Wiggily had a good time, and if the clothes pin doesn't pinch the pillow case so hard that it tickles the bedspread and makes it sneeze all the feathers out, I'll tell you next about Uncle Wiggily and the White Queen.

CHAPTER XXII

UNCLE WIGGILY AND THE WHITE QUEEN

Uncle Wiggily Longears, the nice rabbit gentleman, was hopping along through the woods one day, wondering if he would have an adventure with Alice of Wonderland or some of her friends, when, all of a sudden, coming to a place where a rail fence ran along among the trees he saw, caught in a crack of one of the rails by its legs, a white butterfly.

The poor butterfly was fluttering its wings, trying to pull out its legs, but it had to pull very gently, for a butterfly's leg, you know, is very tender and easily broken, like a piece of spider-web.

"Oh, my!" cried kind Uncle Wiggily, when he saw what was the matter. "You are in trouble, aren't you? I'm glad I happened to come along."

"Why are you glad; to see me in trouble?" asked the white butterfly.

"No, indeed!" exclaimed the bunny uncle. "But I want to help you."

"Well, I wish you would," went on the fluttering creature. "I've tried and tried again to get my poor leg loose, but I can't. And I'm on my way—oh, but I forgot. That part is a secret!" quickly said the butterfly.

"Well, then, don't tell me," spoke Uncle Wiggily with a laugh, "for I might not be very good at keeping secrets. But I'll soon have your leg loose."

With that he took the small end of his red, white and blue striped rheumatism crutch that Nurse Jane Fuzzy Wuzzy had gnawed for him out of a cornstalk and putting the little end of his crutch in the crack of the rail fence, Uncle Wiggily gave a hard push, opened the crack wider, and soon the butterfly's leg was loose and she could fly away.

"But first I must thank you, Uncle Wiggily," she said. "And as you did me so great a favor I want to do you one in return. Not now, perhaps, as I am in a hurry, but later. So if ever you find you want something you can't get, just come to these woods and say a little verse. Then you shall have your wish."

"What verse shall I say?" asked Uncle Wiggily.

"This," answered the butterfly. Then she recited:

"When the wind blows in the trees,

Making perfume for the breeze,

Will you grant to me this boon,

That my wish may come true soon?"

"And what then?" asked the bunny.

"Then," answered the butterfly, "you must whisper your wish to a green leaf and — well, we'll see what happens next."

"Thank you," said Uncle Wiggily, and then he hopped on through the woods while the butterfly fluttered away.

Uncle Wiggily had no adventure that day, but when he reached home to his hollow stump bungalow he found his muskrat lady housekeeper in the kitchen looking quite sad and blue.

"Well, Nurse Jane Fuzzy Wuzzy!" cried the jolly bunny uncle. "Whatever is the matter?"

"Oh, I have broken my nice gold and diamond dishpan, and I can't do any more kitchen work until it is mended. I can't wash the dishes nor get you any supper."

"Oh, never mind about that," said Uncle Wiggily. "I'll take the diamond dishpan down to the five and ten cent store and have them mend it for you. Where is it?"

Nurse Jane gave it to him. The pan had a big crack right across the middle. The muskrat lady said it had fallen to the floor and had broken when she went to get Jackie Bow Wow, the little puppy dog boy a slice of bread and jam.

"I'll soon have it fixed for you," said Uncle Wiggily. But it was more easily said than done. The five and ten cent store was closed because every one was on a picnic, and no one else could mend the dishpan.

"Never mind, I'll buy Nurse Jane a new one and say nothing about it," said Uncle Wiggily. "I'll surprise her."

But this, too, was more easily said than done. In all Woodland, where Uncle Wiggily and the animal folk lived, there was not another gold and diamond dishpan to be had. They were all sold.

"Oh, dear! What shall I do?" thought Uncle Wiggily. "Nurse Jane will be so unhappy!" Then he happened to think of the white butterfly and what she had told him. So, taking the dishpan, he went to the wood where he had helped the fluttering creature and whispered to a leaf the little verse:

"When the wind blows in the trees,

Making perfume for the breeze,

Will you grant to me this boon,

That my wish may come true soon?"

"Well, what is your wish?" asked a sudden voice.

"I wish Nurse Jane's gold and diamond dishpan to be mended," said Uncle Wiggily.

Instantly something white came fluttering down out of a tree, and the bunny saw it was the white butterfly. And then, all of a sudden, before he could count up to sixteen thousand, the white butterfly seemed to fade away and in its place was a beautiful White Queen, seated on a golden throne with a diamond crown on her head.

"You shall have your wish, Uncle Wiggily," she said. "Give me the dishpan."

"Why—why!" exclaimed the bunny. "You are—you are—"

"I am the White Queen from Alice in Wonderland," was the answer, "and I will ask you a riddle. When you take the dishes out of the pan what remains?"

"Nothing," answered the bunny.

"Wrong," answered the White Queen. "The water does. Now I'll mend this for you." And she did, taking some gold from her throne and some diamonds from her crown to mend the broken dishpan.

Soon Nurse Jane's pan was as good as ever and she could wash the dishes in it.

"Thank you," said Uncle Wiggily. "But how is it you are a queen and a butterfly, too?"

"Oh, we Queens lead a sort of butterfly existence," said the White Queen. "But I must go now, for I have to find the tarts for the Queen of Hearts who is always losing hers."

Then, changing herself into a white butterfly again, the Queen flew away, and Uncle Wiggily, with the mended dishpan, hopped on to his hollow stump bungalow, where he and Nurse Jane were soon having a nice supper and were very happy.

And if the potato masher doesn't go to the moving pictures and step on the toes of the egg beater I'll tell you next about Uncle Wiggily and the Red Queen.

CHAPTER XXIII

UNCLE WIGGILY AND THE RED QUEEN

Once upon a time, when Uncle Wiggily Longears, the rabbit gentleman, was out walking in the woods, he stopped beside a little hole in the ground near a pile of oak tree leaves, and listening, when the wind stopped blowing, he heard a little voice saying:

"Oh, but where can she be? I fear she is lost! Little Crawlie is lost!"

"My! That's too bad," thought Uncle Wiggily. "Somebody's little girl is lost. I must ask if I cannot help find her." So he called:

"Oh, ho, there! May I have the pleasure of helping you in your trouble, whoever you are?"

"But who are you?" asked a voice that seemed to come out of the little hole in the ground.

"I am Uncle Wiggily Longears," answered the bunny. "You can easily see me, but I can't see you. And who is this Crawlie who is lost?"

"She is my little girl," was the answer, and up the hole in the ground came crawling a red ant lady, who was crying tear drops about as large as that part of a pin point which you can't see but can only feel.

"Oh, my!" exclaimed Uncle Wiggily. "I couldn't imagine who would live in such a little house, but of course ants can. And now what about Crawlie?"

"She is my little girl," answered the red ant. "I sent her to the store about an hour ago to get a loaf of sand bread, but she hasn't come back and I'm sure something has happened to her."

"Let us hope not," spoke Uncle Wiggily, softly. "I'll go at once and look for her. Have no fear, Mrs. Ant. I'll find Crawlie for you. It is rather a queer name."

"Crawlie is called that because she crawls in such a funny way," said Mrs. Ant. "Oh, dear! I hope she is all right. If she should happen to have fallen down a crack in a peach stone she'd never get out."

"I'll find her," said Uncle Wiggily, bravely.

So off started the bunny uncle, hopping on his red, white and blue striped rheumatism crutch over the fields and through the woods, looking for Crawlie.

He had not gone very far before he heard a small voice calling:

"Help! Help! Oh, will no one help me?"

"Yes, of course, I will!" answered the bunny, and then he saw an acorn which seemed to be moving along the ground in a queer way.

"Ha! Can it be that this acorn is alive?" asked Uncle Wiggily. "And can that acorn want help?" he cried.

"No, it is I — Crawlie, the ant girl — under the acorn," was the answer, "and I want help, for I'm in such trouble."

"What kind?" asked Uncle Wiggily. "What's the trouble?"

"Why, I'm caught under this acorn here and I can't get out," was the answer, and Crawlie's voice sounded as though she had gone down cellar to get a crumb of apple and couldn't find her way back again. "I went under the acorn shell, which is empty," said the little ant girl, "and though it was nicely propped up on one side when I crawled in, it was blown over by the wind and I was held beneath it. Oh, dear! I can't get out and go to the store for the loaf of sand bread!"

"Oh, yes you can!" cried jolly Uncle Wiggily. "I'll lift the acorn shell off you and let you out."

So he did, easily picking up the empty oak tree acorn from where it was covering Crawlie, and then the little ant girl, who was red, just like her mother, could walk about.

"Oh, thank you, Uncle Wiggily," she said. "If ever we ants can do you a favor we will."

"Oh, pray do not mention it," spoke Uncle Wiggily, modest-like and shy. Then Crawlie hurried on to the sand bread store and the bunny hopped along over the fields and through the woods.

He had not gone very far before he met a poor old June bug gentleman, and the June bug seemed very sad and unhappy.

"What is the matter?" asked Uncle Wiggily.

"Lots," was the answer. "You see it is now time, being July, for June bugs like myself to get in their winter wood so we will not freeze in the cold weather. But I hurt my legs, banging into an electric light one night, and I'm so lame and stiff that I can't gather any wood at all. I shall freeze, I know I shall!" and the June bug gentleman was more sad than ever.

"Oh, cheer up!" cried Uncle Wiggily. "There is plenty of wood under these trees. I'll help you gather it."

"There is no need to do that," said another voice, and, looking up, Uncle Wiggily and the June bug saw, sitting on a green mossy log, a Red Queen wearing a golden crown.

"Oh!" exclaimed Uncle Wiggily in surprise. "You are—"

"I am the Red Queen from Alice in Wonderland," interrupted the lady on the log. "I was also the red ant lady who was crying and also Crawlie, the red ant girl. You were so kind to me when you thought I was only a crawling insect that now, when I have changed myself into a Red Queen, I want to help you. And I know I can best help you by helping this June bug friend of yours."

"Indeed, you can!" said Uncle Wiggily, thankful like.

"I thought so," spoke the Red Queen. "Watch!"

With that she waved her magic wand, and, instantly, ten million red, white and black ants came crawling out of old logs from holes in the ground and from under piles of leaves, and each ant took up a little stick of wood and carried it into the June bug's house for him, so he had plenty of wood for all winter, and couldn't freeze.

"There you are, Uncle Wiggily!" laughed the Red Queen. "One kindness, you see, makes another," and then she got in her golden chariot and drove away, and when the June bug gentleman had thanked him, and the ants had crawled home, the bunny himself went to his hollow stump bungalow very happy.

And if the looking glass doesn't make faces at the hairbrush and knock the teeth out of the comb so it can't have fun and bite the talcum powder, I'll tell you next about Uncle Wiggily and Tweedledum.

CHAPTER XXIV

UNCLE WIGGILY AND TWEEDLEDUM

"Are you in, Uncle Wiggily?" asked a voice at the hollow stump bungalow one morning, and the rabbit gentleman looked up to see Alice from Wonderland standing on the door sill.

"Yes, of course I'm in, my dear," he answered. "Can't you see me?"

"I can't be sure of anything I see," answered the little girl with flaxen hair, "especially since I've been having so many queer adventures. I used to think I saw the Cheshire cat, when it was only his grin smiling at me. And maybe now I'm only looking at your ears, or tall silk hat, and thinking it's you."

"No, I'm here all right," answered the bunny. "Is there anything I can do for you?"

"Yes," answered Alice. "I'd like you to come for a walk with me. I haven't much longer time to stay with you, and I want to have all the fun I can."

"Are you going away?" asked Uncle Wiggily.

"I have very soon to go back in the book where I belong," answered Alice. "But no matter. Come now, and we'll go look for an adventure."

So Alice and Uncle Wiggily started off over the fields and through the woods, and they had not gone very far before they suddenly heard, among the trees, some voices crying:

"You did it!"

"No, I didn't!"

"Yes, you did; you know you did!"

"No, I didn't! I know I didn't!"

"Well, we'll have to have a battle, anyhow!"

And then came a sound as if some one was beating a carpet with a fishing pole and voices cried:

"Oh! Oh, dear! Ouch! Oh, how it hurts!"

"My, what in the world can that be?" asked Uncle Wiggily. "It sounds like an adventure all right."

"I think it is," answered Alice. "It's probably Tweedledum and Tweedledee fighting."

"Fighting? Tweedledee and Tweedledum?" asked the surprised bunny.

"Oh, it's only in fun," laughed Alice, "and they have to do it because it's that way in the book, for if they didn't things wouldn't come out right. Yes, there they are." And she pointed off through the trees, where Uncle Wiggily saw two round, fat, little boys, dressed exactly the same, and looking so like one another that no one could tell them apart, except when they were together—just like twins, you know.

"Oh, I'm so glad to see you!" called Alice to the two queer fat chaps. They were as round as barrels, both of them. Uncle Wiggily noticed that on the collar of one was the word DUM, while on the other was the word DEE.

"Tweedle, the rest of their name, is on the back of their collars," Alice explained. "As it's the same for both, they didn't need it in front."

Then the fat boys turned around, like tops slowly spinning, and, surely enough, on the back of the white collar of each were letters spelling TWEEDLE.

"I'm glad to see you," spoke Uncle Wiggily. "I heard you—sort of—er—well, you know," he went on, diffident-like, not wishing to say he had heard the brothers quarreling.

"Oh, it's all right, we do that every day," said Tweedledee.

"And, contrariwise, twice on Sunday," added Tweedledum. "We have to for the verse about us says:

"'Tweedledum and Tweedledee

Agreed to have a battle;

For Tweedledum said Tweedledee

Had spoiled his nice new rattle.

"'Just then down flew a monstrous crow,

As black as a tar barrel,

   Which frightened both the heroes so,

They quite forgot their quarrel.'"

"Only we weren't really frightened," said Tweedledee. "We just made believe so, and laughed at the crow. And I didn't really spoil Tweedledum's nice new rattle, for here it is now," and taking his arm down from around his brother's neck he took the rattle from his pocket and shook it, making a noise like a drum.

And, just as he did that, all of a sudden, out from behind a big stump came—not a monstrous crow, but the bad old skillery-scalery alligator, who cried:

"Ah, ha! At last I have him! Now I'll get that Uncle Wiggily Longears chap! Ah, ha!" and he made a grab for the gentleman bunny.

"Oh, dear!" exclaimed Alice. "Please don't hurt Uncle Wiggily!"

"Yes, I shall!" snapped the 'gator. "I'll bumble him and mumble him, that's what I'll do."

"Oh, no you won't!" exclaimed Tweedledum, wabbling toward the alligator as Jimmie Wibblewobble, the boy duck, waddled when he walked.

"I won't what?" asked the 'gator.

"You won't bumble or mumble Uncle Wiggily. First you have to catch me!"

"Pooh! That's easily done," snapped the alligator. "You are so fat that you can't run any more than a rubber ball."

"Will you promise to let Uncle Wiggily alone until you catch me?" asked Tweedledum, eagerly.

"I promise," said the alligator smiling to himself, for he thought he could easily catch the fat twin, and his promise wouldn't count.

"Then here I go! Catch me!" suddenly cried Tweedledum. And with that he stretched out on the ground and began to roll down hill in the woods.

And as he was fat and round he rolled as fast as a rubber ball, and he rolled so fast (ever so much faster than if he had run) that when the alligator raced after him, as he had promised he would do, why the bad double-jointed skillery-scalery creature got all out of breath and couldn't bumble or mumble a strawberry, to say nothing of Uncle Wiggily. And the 'gator didn't catch the fat boy either.

So Tweedledum, rolling down hill that way, which he could do much better than walking or running, saved the bunny uncle from the alligator, and Mr. Longears was very glad, and so was Alice.

And if the knife and fork don't go to the candy store, just when supper is ready, and make the spoon holder wait for them before eating the ice cream, I'll tell you next about Uncle Wiggily and Tweedledee.

CHAPTER XXV
UNCLE WIGGILY AND TWEEDLEDEE

"Oh, Uncle Wiggily!" cried a voice, as the old rabbit gentleman started out from his hollow stump bungalow one morning to walk in the woods and look for an adventure. "Oh, Uncle Wiggily, be careful!"

"Be careful of what, if you please, and who are you, if I may ask?" politely inquired the bunny.

"I am your friend Alice, from Wonderland," was the answer, "and I want you to be careful and not get hurt today."

"I always am careful," answered Uncle Wiggily. "I look for cabbage and turnip traps wherever I go, and I never pick up a bit of carrot on the Woodland path without first making sure there is no string fast to it, to catch me. What do you mean, Alice?" he asked the little flaxen-haired girl as she came out of the bushes and sat down on the stoop of the hollow stump bungalow. "What do you mean?"

"I don't know just what I do mean, Uncle Wiggily," said Alice. "But last night I dreamed you were in trouble and I could not help you. I felt so sorry! As soon as I woke up this morning I hurried over to tell you to be careful."

"Oh, I'll be careful," promised the bunny gentleman. "But in your dream did no one help me?"

"Yes, after a while two funny little fat boys did," answered Alice. "But I don't remember that part of my dream. However, if you are going for a walk I'll go with you and do what I can in case the Jabberwocky or the Hop Scotch bird try to chase you."

"The Hop Scotch isn't a bird," said Uncle Wiggily, with a laugh that made his pink nose twinkle like the strawberry on top of a cheese cake. "It's a bit of candy."

"Oh, Uncle Wiggily! It's a game!" cried Susie Littletail, the rabbit girl, coming out from behind a stump just then. "It's a game where you jump around on the pavement, and if you and Alice are going to play it, please may I watch you?"

"We aren't going to play," said Alice. "It's long past play time."

"I am going to look for an adventure," said Uncle Wiggily.

"Then, please, may I come?" begged Susie. "I'll help look."

"Come along!" cried jolly Uncle Wiggily and soon the three of them were on their way through the woods.

They had not gone very far, over the paths with the big green ferns on either side, when, all of a onceness out from behind a big log jumped the two bad old skillery-scalery alligators, one with the humps on his tail and the other with his tail all double-jointed, so he could wiggle it seven ways from Sunday.

"Ah, ha!" cried the hump-tailed 'gator.

"Ha, ha!" cried the double-jointed one. "At last we have caught you!" and they both made a grab for the rabbit gentleman, one catching him on the left side and the other on the right, and holding him fast.

"Oh!" cried Uncle Wiggily. "Oh, dear! Please let me go!"

"No!" snapped the first 'gator. And "No!" snapped the second, both flapping their tails.

"Oh, this is my dream! This is my dream!" said Alice, sadly. "But where are the two fat boys that saved Uncle Wiggily. Where are they?"

"Here is one, if you please," answered a voice, and out stepped Tweedledee, the queer little fat chap from the Alice in Wonderland book. "I'll help you, Uncle Wiggily."

"Thank you, very much," spoke the rabbit gentleman. "If you would kindly make these alligators let me go — "

"Pooh! Huh! Humph! What! Him make us let you go? Well, I should say NOT!" sniffed the first alligator.

"The very idea" sneered the second. "It will take a great deal more than one fat boy to make us let go of a nice, fat, juicy rabbit once we have caught him. Certainly NOT!"

"Ahem! How about TWO fat boys?" suddenly asked another voice, and there stood another beside Tweedledee, a fat boy, who looked just the same exactly; even as you seem to yourself when you peek at your reflection in the bath room mirror.

"No, we won't let you go for two fat boys, either," said the double-jointed alligator, while Alice murmured:

"Oh, this is my dream! This is my dream! I wish I could remember how it came out!"

"Was Uncle Wiggily saved?" asked Susie Littletail in a whisper.

"Yes," said Alice.

"Then it's all right," spoke the rabbit girl.

"Let Uncle Wiggily go!" cried Tweedledee in his most grown-up sort of voice.

"Yes, let him go at once!" added Tweedledum.

"No, indeed!" snapped both alligators together like twins, only, of course, they weren't.

"Well, then," went on Tweedledee, "don't you dare to take away or hurt him unless you guess which are our names. Now tell me truly who am I? And, remember, if you don't guess right, you can't have Uncle Wiggily!"

"You are Tweedledum," said the hump-tailed 'gator.

"No, he is Tweedledee," said the other 'gator. "The one standing next to him is Tweedledum. I guess I ought to know!"

"You're wrong," said the hump-tailed 'gator. "The one I saw first is Tweedledum. I guess I ought to know!"

"I know better!" the double-jointed alligator declared. "He is Tweedledee!"

"Tweedledum!" shouted the other 'gator.

"Tweedledee!" snapped his chum. And then they both began disputing, calling each other names, and throwing mud at one another, until, finally, they were so mixed up about Tweedledum and Tweedledee that they let go of Uncle Wiggily and began shaking their claws at one another, so the rabbit gentleman and Alice and Susie (as well as the two fat boys who looked exactly alike) ran safely away and the bunny was saved, just as Alice had dreamed.

"And to think, if the alligators had only looked at our collars, they would have seen our right names," Tweedledum laughed.

"Of course," said Tweedledee.

But everything came out all right and the alligators only had sawdust for supper. And if the wash lady doesn't take my best collar button to fasten the tablecloth to the ironing board in the clothes basket, I'll tell you next about Uncle Wiggily and the pool of tears.

CHAPTER XXVI

UNCLE WIGGILY AND THE TEAR POOL

Uncle Wiggily Longears, the nice rabbit gentleman, was out walking in the woods one day, wondering what sort of an adventure he would have when he saw a little path, leading away from his hollow stump bungalow, and it seemed to go through a part of the forest in which he had never before been.

"I'll take that path and see where it leads," said the bunny gentleman to himself.

So, taking a piece of ribbon grass, which grew near a clump of ferns, he tied his tall silk hat firmly on his head, leaving his ears sticking out of the holes at the top, and tucking under his paw his red, white and blue striped barber pole rheumatism crutch that Nurse Jane Fuzzy Wuzzy, his muskrat lady housekeeper, had gnawed for him out of a cornstalk, away started Uncle Wiggily.

It was a nice warm summer day, and before the old gentleman bunny had gone very far he began to feel thirsty, just as you do when you go on a picnic and eat pickles, only I hope you don't eat too many of them.

"I wonder if there is not a spring of water around here?" thought Uncle Wiggily, and he began to look about under the low branches of the trees and bushes, at the same time listening for the laughing murmur of a brook flowing over green, mossy stones.

Then Uncle Wiggily sniffed with his pink, twinkling nose until it looked like a chicken picking up corn.

"Ah, ha!" cried the bunny uncle, "I smell water!" for you know animals and birds can smell water when they cannot see it, in which they are more gifted than are we.

So Uncle Wiggily sniffed and sniffed, and then, holding his pink, twinkling nose straight in front of him and letting it go on ahead, instead of lagging behind, he followed it until it led him straight to a little pool of water that was sparkling in the sun, while green moss ferns and bushes grew all around.

"Oh, what a fine spring!" cried the bunny, "And how thirsty I am!"

Mr. Longears, which I call him when first I introduce him to any strangers — Mr. Longears was just going to take a long drink from the pool, or spring, when he happened to notice a little piece of white birch bark tied with a bit of grass to a fern that grew near the water.

"Ha! I wonder if that is a notice not to trespass, or not to fish or hunt, and to keep off the grass, or no admittance except on business or something like that?" thought Uncle Wiggily, as he put on his glasses to see if there was any writing on the birch bark, which animal folk use as we use paper. And there was some writing on the bark. It read:

"Please do not jump in, or drink until I come. Alice from Wonderland."

"Ha! That is strange," thought Uncle Wiggily. "Alice must have been here and put up that sign. But I wonder why she did it? If she knew how warm and thirsty I was she would not make me wait until she came to get a drink. Perhaps it is all a joke, and not her writing at all. One of the bad skillery-scalery alligators or the fuzzy fox may have put up the sign to fool me."

But when the rabbit gentleman took a second look at the birch bark sign he saw that it really was Alice's writing.

"Well, she must have some reason for it," said the bunny, with a sigh. "She dreamed right about two fat boys — Tweedledum and Tweedledee — saving me from the alligators, so she must have some reason for asking me to wait until she comes. But I am very thirsty."

Uncle Wiggily sat down on the green, mossy bank beside the spring of water and looked at it. And it seemed so cool and wet, and he was so thirsty, that it was all he could do to keep from jumping in and having a bath, as well as drinking all he wanted.

The sun grew hotter and more hot, and the rabbit gentleman more and more thirsty, and he didn't know what to do when, all of a sudden, out from the bushes jumped a bad old black bear.

"Ah, ha!" growled the bear. "I am just in time, I see!" and he ran his red tongue over his white teeth as though giving it a trolley ride in a baby carriage.

"In time for what?" asked Uncle Wiggily, casual like and make-believe indifferent.

"In time for lunch," answered the bear. "I was afraid I'd be a little late. I hope I haven't kept you waiting."

"For my lunch?" asked Uncle Wiggily.

"No. For MINE!" and once more the bear smacked his lips hungry like. "I am just in time, I see."

"Oh, I thought you meant you were just in time to take a drink of this water," said the bunny, pointing at the pool. "If you did, you aren't."

"If I did I aren't? What kind of talk is that?" asked the bear, curious like.

"I mean we can't have a drink until Alice comes — the sign says so," spoke Uncle Wiggily, politely.

"Pooh! I don't believe in signs," snapped the bear. "I'm thirsty and I'm going to have a drink," and with that he took a long one from the woodland pool. And then a funny thing happened.

The bear began to grow smaller and smaller. First he was the size of a dog, then of a cat, then of a kitten, then he shrank to the littleness of a mouse, and next he was like a June bug. Then he became a July bug, next he was no larger than a little black ant, and finally he became a microbe, and Uncle Wiggily couldn't see him at all.

"Well, thank goodness he's gone!" said the bunny. "But what made him so shrinking like I wonder?"

"It was the pool of tears," said a voice behind the bunny, and there stood Alice from Wonderland. "This pool is sour alum water, Uncle Wiggily," she said, "and if you drink it you shrink and shrivel up and blow away. That's why I put up the sign so nothing would happen to you. I knew about the pool, as it's in my story book. And now we can go have some funny adventures."

And away they went over the hills and far away and that bear was never seen again. But if your cat doesn't catch the ice cream cone in the mosquito net and feed it to the gold fish, I'll tell you more of Uncle Wiggily's adventures in a little while. For the old gentleman rabbit had many surprising things happen to him. You may read about them in another book to be called "Uncle Wiggily In Fairyland," which tells of some of the Genii and Gnomes of the Arabian Nights.

So, until I have that book ready for you, I'll just wish you a Good-night and many, many happy dreams!

THE END

Milton Keynes UK
Ingram Content Group UK Ltd.
UKHW042313020823
426203UK00004B/256